Jay

and

Robin

Five for Silver

Cathy Cade

Map of the counties

Contents

Before

The old world had been here before. Scarred by its former lives, it had been little changed by its past apocalypses and annihilations.

Its inhabitants had been less fortunate.

After each apocalypse, life began again, not from where it was interrupted, but neither from its first beginnings, as if some cosmic child were practising its creation skills, deciding what to keep and what to discard.

Recovery took aeons as creatures faced extinction. Some adapted. Some returned to the water or took to the air, finding new ways to communicate with their own kind more or less effectively.

The brightest survivors would devise tools, discover how to tame their world, and how to use it. They'd learn to farm, heal, create, modify, and kill more efficiently.

Knowledge can't be unlearned.

But it can be lost in the smog of burning bridges.

Each civilisation's prophets and scientists had foretold a variety of endings for their world, depending on the information available at the time (and sometimes on their funding). Their predictions included alien invasion, meteor collision, solar cooling, global warming, exhaustion, pollution, fire, flood, famine, war, pestilence…

They weren't all wrong.

The flat county of Tarn and its more scenic neighbours had been known by many names, but their current occupants knew none of those. The Tarnfolk knew little enough of their own history in this plague-ridden, neutral world, and nothing at all of what their species had lost.

Or gained, depending on your point of view.

Part One: Meetings

Cutler's Forge

Jay

Here I was again, counting the hours till tomorrow. As I breathed in the smell of cooling charcoal, my thoughts were already on the road.

Dust motes drifted in the late sunbeams that filtered through the windows of the forge to gleam on the bangles I'd just polished. Earrings were paired on the bench ready for packing, and my silver charms were bagged, to be threaded onto plaited cords when sold. I selected eight silver rings for my fingers (I still had ten in those days) and gathered the rest into a drawstring pouch.

I'd begun to sharpen my knife, ready for the journey, when the door to the house opened and Brook's greying head peered around it.

"There you are, Jay!"

My portly parent advanced into the forge. "Leave all that, now. Folks'll be arriving for the hearthwarming before we're ready." Brows drew together. "I hope next week you'll pay more attention to why we send you to Wenn Fair than you fritter on peddling your trinkets."

I took a breath and said nothing. They still considered my jewellery a timewasting hobby. Although now the family coffers were empty, Kip was beginning to appreciate the extra cash it brought in.

Tarnfolk hadn't valued the blackened metal found under the nearby village of Abby. It was too soft to be of practical use. Otherwise, like the stones that once lay above it, the silver would have been taken by now. It was easy to shape though, and when polished shone bright as the moon. My family thought time spent shaping silver would be better spent crafting cups and cutlery, forging forks, flasks, and farm tools, or burnishing blades.

Brook crossed the workshop to inspect the lanterns collected on Cris's workbench by the yard door.

"Make sure these are outside before the sun goes, can you? Cris is still busy in the kitchen. Most of them should hang around the new door. We'll have the players there, and the dancing."

Tonight's party would be a hearthwarming for new rooms recently added to house Cris and Elm's litter of three, with another on the way. Until now Cutler's Forge had been enough to house former generations, who were less successful than Cris in raising their tarlings. Even my parents had lost a baby between Cris and I, and a later sibling that I barely remember. Which is probably why they'd been so keen to take in Rob and Ira all those years ago, when Ira was too grief-crazed to cope with baby Robin.

The Great Sickness had almost wiped us out, all those generations ago, but now the family was expanding we needed more space to accommodate the grandchildren my parents were so keen to accumulate. The rooms had cost more than expected. If we ever needed more, we'd have to build them ourselves.

Despite my parents' heavy hints and broad smiles whenever Rob came around these days, we were in no hurry to provide them with more grandchildren. Three-

and-two-thirds tarlings in the house were more than enough to be going on with.

Brook was paused to bustle off again. "Get a move on, Jay. The 'lings'll be home from school any minute."

Laying the knife and stone aside, I chose my earrings for the evening and threaded them in before turning my attention to the lamps.

Out in the yard, the sun was slipping behind the stable roof. A scruffy tan and white mongrel was basking in its final rays by the gate. The stray had taken to hanging around the yard and roused himself now to greet me, so I bent to rub his ears. Marmalade, the forge's resident mouser, eyed the crossbreed from a water butt, tail swishing in disapproval.

Brook came to light the braziers, face more flushed even than usual and brow furrowed deeper than a party would justify. A table-end appeared in the new doorway and jammed against the frame, prompting an "Oof" from inside, followed by a hissed, "Oh, for heaven's sake!" Kip, my taller and leaner parent, often lost patience with inanimate objects these days.

The table end lifted again but wavered, until Elm ran from the main front door to help manoeuvre it through the gap. The four of us cleared a bigger space for it between braziers.

Kip's mind was elsewhere. "Jay-bird, have you got that list safe? Don't go off without it."

My fist clenched, but I took a slow breath and relaxed my face and my shoulders as Robin recommended whenever my patience was tested.

Once – just once – I had gone to Wenn Fair without Kip's list of requirements. They found the list on my workbench after I left and had, apparently, spent the fortnight worrying. They'd never let me forget it, even though I brought home everything that was on the damned list. Parental approval is like wealth: quicker to lose than it is to regain.

You'd think by now they could trust me to know what I was doing. I'd been working the Wendale fairs since Cris and Elm started breeding like rabbits. There was more to come.

"See if you can't manage to sweet-talk them Llann merchants into trimming the price a bit," said Brook, "when you go to pay for the metals."

Did Brook not understand how auctions worked? I reminded myself that auctioning hadn't been the norm back when they worked the fair together and cheered up on remembering that cute Llann with the dark eyes I managed to sweet-talk at the spring fair. Nothing to do with the price of metal, though.

I was raring to get away again. Fendle must be the quietest village in Tarn. Nothing ever happened. I knew everyone, and they all knew me. Wendale was only the neighbouring county but it was the furthest I had ever travelled. So far.

Nobody noticed my smile, being too preoccupied with their own thoughts. This hearthwarming would do more than celebrate the new rooms. It would signal to the village that all was well with the Cutlers.

With no money in reserve, it was probably not the best time to take on the biggest order we'd ever been offered, but the opportunity was too good to turn down. We'd be supplying a new inn, currently under construction on the main road out of Fendle. The whole order must be delivered in time for the midwinter festival, or they'd buy at Tarfen instead. Merchants in the county town could supply everything from stock… at a price.

We'd taken a loan to pay for more metal, so I'd be bidding with borrowed money at this autumn's fair. It was a temporary inconvenience. Nobody shared Brook's misgivings. With five of us working on the order, what could go wrong?

Approaching the other end of the yard, Cris's two elder sprogs were home from school with their customary escort.

If they were out of school, so was Robin, their teacher. Rob was the person who knew me best in the world. We'd grown up together. I sent out my thoughts. But Rob's were like thunder, so I withdrew.

Like Brook, Rob was turning prickly as a teasel.

Cris's tarlings were brought home by one of their older cousins, along with any of their friends who wanted to use our yard for a shortcut. The dog ran to meet them, tail waving. I expect they sometimes fed him the remains of their lunch. The group slowed to greet him, and two youngsters at the back slipped into the workshop. The door closed softly behind them.

Cay Elver and Fin Hartwood lived at the far end of the village. Fin was a leggy crane, while Cay was a sturdy, round-faced duck who aspired to crane-dom. Both would be leaving school in a few weeks.

As I opened the workshop door, Fin was prowling the workbenches, hooking long hair back behind ears to inspect Elm's workbench. Cay had found my knife, and stubby hands lifted it with reverence to examine the etched handle.

"This is brill! Did you make it?"

"What are you doing in here?"

"It isn't new. How old were you when you made it?"

"Fifteen, sixteen… a couple of summers more than you." The knife had been my final apprentice task.

Fin took it from Cay and inspected the blade with an air of authority. Slender fingers tested it before approving it with a grunt. Fin's eyes challenged mine as the knife was unhurriedly surrendered. I sensed the pull of a resentful glower beside me but, when I looked, Cay's gaze was, as usual, on Fin. I slipped my knife into its sheath.

"Come on, you two. Out!"

That was when I noticed that a pair of teardrop earrings was missing from my bench.

"Hold on, I'll have the earrings back first."

Cay was a picture of innocence. "What earrings?"

I doubt that Fin looked innocent at birth.

"There were five pairs of those teardrops and now there are four."

Cay's eyes were wide. "Maybe they rolled off the table."

"Both of them? Not one or three? How come none of the others have rolled off the table?" I glanced at the floor, anyway.

Fin moved a cloth and said, "They're here," pointing to where a pair of earrings peeped from under it. I checked the rest of the jewellery was still there and shepherded the pair towards the door.

"The shortcut is through the yard, not the workshop. Don't get lost again."

Not that they'd get the chance. The workshop was usually occupied at this time and otherwise locked.

Only I hadn't locked it.

"Sorry," said Cay, head lowered. Doglike eyes peeked up through pale lashes. On an attractive child it might have looked appealing.

Fin tossed shining hair away from expressionless eyes and nodded a farewell.

Outside, the ragged crossbreed lay crunching a stale crust but jumped away from foot-range when Fin stalked out with Cay paddling behind. Once they were through the gate, he circled to sit by me and watch them out of sight. A blackbird sang from the stable roof, caroling its joy at another day's survival and the promise of tomorrow.

Tomorrow I'd be on the road.

Hearthwarming

Robin

I fought the urge to limp, although no one was watching our progress along School Lane.

It had been a long afternoon. The class was restless and the older ones who would soon be leaving had tried my patience. It happened every year; I could deal with it. But by home time I was tired.

The tarlings must have noticed I was flagging. Two of them helped tidy up without me asking, and closed the window shutters while I locked away the knife I'd used to reshape quill-ends. It was a small knife with my initials carved into the handle. Jay had made it for me.

I had been looking forward to spending this last evening with Jay before the convoy left tomorrow, but now a muscle in my back was protesting at being held for too long where it didn't want to be. My aged parent trudged even slower than I, leaning heavily on a gnarled walking stick and grumbling all the while.

What depravities in a former life had earned me Ira?

On my return from work, I had been met by the mess Fern's pups left after they had escaped from their pen.

I wilted.

"Don't stand there like wheat in a windstorm. Straighten yourself up!" My hands tightened, as did a muscle in my back. "You need to find homes for these pups – the sooner the better."

I had unclenched each finger in turn, feeling blood, sticky from a bitten nail-end that had reopened. Jay nudged at my thoughts but was gone before I could respond. And with the pups to round up and Fern to feed, I had no leisure to go seeking. I told myself we would meet this evening.

The dogs weren't the reason for Ira's bad temper.

Ira didn't want to come out tonight, but sure as sheil wasn't going to let me go alone and enjoy myself. I realised long ago that this has little to do with parental concern and everything to do with control.

Ira never wanted me: an undersized tarling with a kink. I should have been the one who died. Yet I have my uses.

I may not be much, but I'm all Ira has left.

Our sluglike progress in the gathering dusk left me plenty of time to inspect the trees turning russet and purple and gold to one side of the lane, and nature's remedies replenishing themselves around their roots. Undergrowth on the other side was similarly abundant at the edges of the farmer's crop. White smoke drifted across the fields, seasoning the autumn air as the lamps of Cutler's Forge beckoned at the end of School Lane.

Once through the gate, we followed the lanterns to the farthest door while Ira complained about the extra distance. At the open doorway, I straightened my back and shoulders before entering.

Brook was inside, directing operations.

"Ira, Robin, welcome to our hearth. Dusty, take their cloaks."

One of Brook's grandchildren took our cloaks, forgetting (or avoiding) Ira's disgusting hat. Furniture had been moved and mantelpieces decorated since I was there the day before.

"This is lovely, Brook. You must all have worked hard to get it ready."

Ira's eyes puckered to peer into Brook's. "You look knackered. I'm guessing that useless Jay-bird wasn't much help. How's your dodgy knee?"

"Still moving, Ira. Mustn't grumble." Another tarling appeared. "Tam, take Robin's firewood for the stack."

Wood was the traditional gift for hearthwarming. Folklore claimed that sheil sprites were attracted to the warmth of a new fire. A sheil that took up residence would protect the children of the house. Not that the Cutlers were superstitious but, as Brook pointed out, there's no harm in balancing your bets.

I had enjoyed the protection of Cutler's Forge myself as a child. In a sense, I still did. This particular hearth would warm Cris and Elm's 'lings, with a fourth due in the coming year. A celebration was due, even if nobody believed, these days, in the sheil of the hearth (or, indeed, in any of the star-born).

Behind us Sandy Tyke, co-owner of the Barley Mow, ducked through the doorway. Immediately, the room seemed smaller. It was Sandy who had gifted me my hound, Fern. Lamed at birth, she was no use for hunting, but Fern was still a purebred hound.

The same couldn't be said of her pups.

"Hello, Ira love, Robin. How did the whelping go?"

"All well, thank the shiel! It must be just her leg that's deformed. The pups were small though; that would help, wouldn't it?"

"Have you identified the culprit yet?"

I shook my head. "I swear she never went out unwatched the whole time she was in season. They must be shiel-pups. Unless a fox got into the space I'd fenced around her dog-door."

"No, foxes don't breed with dogs, for some reason." Sandy's voice rose. "And how is Ira? We haven't seen you in the Barley Mow lately."

Ira's response was loud, due to encroaching deafness, and carried to half the room.

"What about this new tavern they're building, eh? It's going to take away your trade."

Sandy's answering bark wasn't much quieter.

"I wouldn't have thought so, Ira, out there on the Tarfen road. Why should our regulars walk all that way when we're here for them in the middle of Fendle?"

"Hah!" There was a world of meaning in the outburst, flung like a curse and followed by a prophecy. "I'll be reminding you of that!" The hat flapped crow-like in Ira's pointing hand.

Ira liked to appear more knowledgeable than everyone else, usually with little justification. A few eavesdroppers nodded eloquently, as if confirmed in their own opinion. Others looked sideways at us before moving away.

What would it be like to have an ordinary, inconspicuous parent?

Ira's scorn carried across the room to Kip, earning a sharp glance from the grey eyes which we once believed could read our minds. Jay's eyes were the same pale grey but rarely saw beyond your smile. Even when you wanted them to.

In a community of clans and extended families, Ira was my only blood relation. I never knew my other parent. Sal had died trying to rescue young Aspen from the river in the year I was born.

Kip and Brook had been more like parents to me than Ira ever was.

I scanned the room, sensing Jay was near. Vivid sarongs and tunics clashed merrily, their bright colours an antidote to our dull, serviceable workday wear. I'm as fond of colour as the next Tarn, but I believed back then that quieter shades suited me better, not realising how my olives and ochres stood out among the peacocks.

We followed Ira's nose as the scent of new wood yielded to onion and thyme wafting from the table. Those flagging steps always rallied in the presence of food and drink. Especially drink.

A touch on my right shoulder alerted me to its droop. The fingers that rested on it were long and slender, with too many rings.

"Cheer up, Rob! It may never happen."

I levelled the shoulder while turning. "Maybe that's what I'm afraid of."

Jay smiled back, finding nothing troublesome in my words. Tonight, a whisper of chased silver danced from each ear while a matching pendant lay against smooth skin in the open neck of a ruby kaftan. Jay liked to wear things that shone.

Behind Jay, Mikki Carter was uncharacteristically tidy in azure blue, with a matching blue streak in the straggly, white thatch of hair. Seeing me eyeing the streak, Mikki winked. I mixed the colours for Mikki's hair to match new or re-dyed outfits, but it didn't always turn out so well as this one had.

Mikki was older than us and had supervised Jay's first trip to the Wenn Fair. Ever since then, they travelled together to High Wenn.

We retreated to a corner with our drinks, leaving Ira at the table. Their talk was all of tomorrow's departure. I tried not to dampen their enthusiasm, but I knew we would lose mind-contact as the convoy drew further away. It happened each time Jay left for the fair. I hoped it was caused by the increasing distance.

This trip, Mikki would be taking a new cart, equipped with a different kind of spring devised by Charley Wysmith, a cousin of Jay's. They were simmering, eager to be off.

"The apprentices can travel in your wagon, Jay. You're travelling with me. I want you singing the new cart's praises at High Wenn when everyone else is nursing their bruises."

Jay was bubbling. Thumb and forefinger stroked an earring. "Charley's not risking the trip, then? Afraid a bumpy ride might start the baby early, I suppose."

I was beginning to realise what these new springs might mean. "If the cart's as smooth as Mikki says, and doesn't joggle my back, I'd be able to come too."

Jay hesitated.

Mikki said, "Well, we could do with someone sensible to keep proper track of the contracts. After an evening chatting up the Llann and drinking their grog, I can hardly remember my name next morning, never mind what we've agreed the night before."

I'd caught an impression of trapped animal before Jay's shield went up. "You wouldn't leave your apprentice to manage the school without you for three weeks though."

"Kip would help out."

I reminded Mikki, "Kip was a teacher back in Tarlake."

It was Kip who had persuaded the Administrators that I could do the job, having been a teacher before coming to Fendle. It was also Kip who mentored me through the first year to make sure I could.

Jay frowned. "That was a lifetime ago."

Why should I feel I needed to back up my case?

Heat rose to my cheeks, and my scalp prickled. "Anyone would think you didn't want me to come."

Mikki made a tactical withdrawal. "I'll go for more barley wine."

"Don't be silly, Rob. It's just that… the new springs haven't been tested yet. Not long-distance." Jay's shoulders relaxed. "And I can't see you trekking to High Wenn if bits start falling off on the way."

The smile was back, but Jay's thoughts were still shielded.

The mind-bonds our school friends shared with siblings and parents had all faded as they grew to adulthood. I'd told myself that ours endured because we were soulmates, destined to be partners through life.

Lately, I wondered if our bond was, after all, a hangover from our childhood as foster-sibs, that survived only because Jay hadn't grown up yet.

Fans and Foes

Jay

Between Ira and a sore back, Robin was in a mood and now was sore with me too.

The clear notes of a flute sounded out in the yard, followed by pipe and fiddle. A few squeaks and squeals later, they got each other's measure and fell into a rhythm. Robin brightened. Music always did that.

"I'm going outside. Are you coming?"

I said, "You go on. I'll fetch my lute."

Then I spotted a chance to earn myself some credit. "I'll take a drink to Ira first, before one of the 'lings tops up that empty beaker with ale."

It was a penance. We didn't get on. To Ira, I was still the tarling who'd led Rob into tree-climbing or tiddler-fishing or anything that might make life more fun. But someone had to make sure Ira's drinks were watered, or we'd have to carry the old goblin home.

Kip had also spotted the empty beaker. We arrived together with our blackberry cordials. These were dismissed at a sip and wrinkles gathered deeper around the pursed mouth.

Rob had been born with a crooked back. Not long after the birth, Ira's partner drowned trying to rescue their firstborn from the river. The triple blow was enough to unhinge a mind that was already unstable – or so people said. My grandparents were worried for the baby and suggested Ira and Robin should stay at the forge for a while. "A while" turned out to be seventeen years.

Ira wasn't here for old time's sake though. The old soak had come for a drink, or several, and was ready to leave if more wasn't forthcoming – and drag Rob home too. I stroked a silver earring for inspiration. It would be easier to change the river's flow than change Ira's mind.

But Kip relished a challenge. "The dancing's just starting, and you know how Robin loves the dancing."

"Can't think why! What's the point watching and not joining in? I'm ready for my bed and the sooner, the better. We'll be off now."

"If you're tired Ira, why don't I walk you back to the cottage?" said Kip, "and when they cut the hearthwarming cake, Robin can bring some home for you."

It had been a while since the last Fendle hearthwarming, and Ira had forgotten about the customary mead-soaked hearthwarming cake.

Above the grizzled head, Kip's eyes, level with mine, were a little too wide. "Jay, I think there's a flask of that blackberry wine in the pantry. Go see if you can find it, for Ira to take home."

I nodded and went to fill an empty flask with watered wine and berry juice, while Kip stood ready with Ira's stick and battered hat.

We found Rob outside. The moon was full in a cold sky, but lamps and torches flickered with warmth. Dancers circled between glowing braziers, their smoke tasting of burnt wood and seared herbs. The leave-taking was curtailed when Robin rashly spoke of coming to the next fair.

Ira was appalled beyond speech. Fortunately.

Kip took advantage of the lull to steer the unresisting bulk homewards while pointing out that anything might happen before spring. Once on the road, Ira's power of speech returned.

"I don't trust that one out of sight. Its left hand dunno what the right hand's up to. It's time Jay Cutler found someone else to settle with. The sooner, the better."

A further tally of my shortcomings rang out like judgement as the figures receded into darkness, each accusation punctuated by the thump of the walking stick.

A number of guests paused to listen.

Taz Fletcher and Jessmund Giltin were a formidable pair. As Fendle's Administrators they spent most of their time at Tarfen, where the Assemblies sat in buildings that had once housed the Chief Family. This week both Minstrers were back in Fendle. They arrived as Ira was leaving and lingered by a brazier to enjoy the fading invective.

Jess's smile was wide, discoloured teeth blending with the dark gaps between them. Chins wobbled at each titter. Jess could be difficult to escape, standing too close and wheezing noxious gusts or patting my shoulder and forgetting to remove the hand.

Taz was a substantial figure too, but bovine to Jess's pork. Neither had noticed us yet, so I pulled Rob into the shadows, where we waited for them to continue into the house.

Jess watched Ira's shadow departing. "If I were young Robin, I'd put hemlock in that one's tea, hmph. Ira always was an unforgiving beggar... though it never seemed to bother Sal," eyes glazing at the memory. "I suppose you can overlook a lot when your partner looks like Ira did back then." Focus returned to the receding lamp. "…Although it's hard to believe it now."

Taz turned, ready to move on. "Did you know them well?"

"The Hawns always kept to themselves. They lived well enough; the Sickness had culled their competition. They were the only apothecaries left in three villages." A knowing nod set jowls trembling. "It was common knowledge old Hawn had a fat cushion put aside for a bumpy ride. Course, Sal insisted they'd settled for love, and when the old skinflint died, the pair claimed there never was any money."

A snort of derision conveyed Jess's opinion of that. "Ira and Robin are the only Hawns left now. They're probably sitting on the family fortune in that School Lodge. Hmph."

Beside me in the darkness, Rob was gnawing at a fingernail as Jess rubbed blubbery hands together in the warmth of the brazier.

Taz's grey head shook. "Mm, I'd heard the rumour, but they certainly don't live like barons. If it ever was true, I don't think there'd be anything left now. Ira stopped working when Sal died, and nobody can live on thin air."

"They can when someone else is feeding them. The Cutlers kept them all those years. I'll wager the old beggar has a nice little stash hidden away in that cottage they're living in free."

Rob had heard enough and stepped forward, like a bantam squaring for a fight. I had to follow. Taz was first to see us emerge from the shadows behind Jess.

"Good evening, Robin, Jay. Keeping well, I hope?"

Jess stiffened before turning.

Robin said, "Good evening, Administrator Fletcher. Surely, you've not come all this way for the hearthwarming?"

Taz said, "Just a routine visit to the school, Robin, to see how your young apprentice is doing. We'll be sure to drop in on your class first before we go into Ty's."

Rob's dismay was quickly masked.

Jess had recovered from any embarrassment and oozed closer. "Jay, my dear, how nice to see you! How are your parents?" Both hands clasped one of mine.

Robin came to my rescue. "Brook is inside, Administrator Giltin, and Kip won't be long. I'm sure they'll be pleased to see you."

"Jess, please. No formality here."

The old letch was treated to Rob's best hundred-candle smile. "I'm afraid I'm going to drag Jay away now to dance. Come on Jay!"

Rob had no intention of dancing, but I was grateful to be dragged away.

The Party's Over

Robin

Jay told me I should join in the dancing. "Don't worry about other people. Nobody's watching."

People who say that know damn well everyone's watching *them* when they dance. Jay was an amazing dancer, stepping out confidently. Even when the steps were wrong. It was a delight and a torment to watch as dancers took their turn in the middle of the set. I coveted those hips.

Music always lifts my spirits. I sensed Jay's relief and felt the thought shield relax. Music and rhythm did that for Jay too. A love of music was one of the things we shared.

When the dancing was over and the songs all sung, Jay went to exchange the lute for a lamp to light my way home. Meanwhile, some guests who were loath to depart sang on, while others helped clear the yard. Jay returned to find me collecting plates and beakers.

"Leave those and tell me what you think of these." A small cloth pouch was dropped into my palm, and I pulled the draw-string loose to peer in. "I made them with you in mind, so you'd better have a pair before I sell them all."

Jay often gave me earrings, but these were different – from each other, that is. I mostly wore a single earring in my left ear, although both had been pierced as a child, the same as everyone else. One of this pair was a delicate silver sun with wavy rays, and the other a curving new moon.

"You can wear them on different days or, if you ever change your mind, you can wear them together."

"Jay, they're perfect!"

I took the hoop from my left ear and replaced it with the dangling moon, dropping my silver hoop into the pouch.

"The sun can bring me luck tomorrow for the Minstrers' visit."

"If it's a talisman you need, perhaps Ira can plait you a straw doll."

I ignored this reference to village rumours that surrounded Ira and took the lamp to lead us out of the yard. I sang along with the chorus that had just begun, and Jay joined in, harmonising in a clear, sweet voice that moved you to forgive the singer almost anything.

Away from the braziers I might have shivered.

"Don't you have a coat?"

"I came in a cloak, but it's gone. Ira must have taken it."

"Have my coat. I'm still warm from the last reel."

It was already over my shoulders. I set down the lamp and fumbled my arms into its sleeves. Jay fastened the front and retrieved the lamp. "You know, that suits you."

"It's a nice coat," I said. "Your clothes always are." Jay had an eye for beautiful things, although I doubted it was this snug on its owner.

"It gives you a waist. You should tailor your clothes more."

Did I want a waist? "Mine's lopsided."

"You need to stop running yourself down." Jay was good at telling me what I needed. "Your kink isn't as obvious as you think it is." It felt obvious. Especially when it made my back ache. "It needn't stop you doing anything you want."

I grunted. "That's easy for you to say. You forget about my other disability. Ira isn't supportive like your parents."

"D'you think so? They support you, but they don't have much faith in me." Already, I recognised what was about to follow. "They want me settled, like Cris, with half a dozen tarlings. I can't be trusted to know what's good for me."

The snort that followed might have accompanied a colt's stamping hoof, but Jay had at least stopped the foot-stamping in recent years.

"What do you think is good for you, then?"

Jay fingered an earring. "I've no idea, to be honest." I waited. "I'd like to travel. Not just to the fair – all over. Every day is the same here – same flat scenery, same old routine, same faces. Nobody *wants* to change anything. Everybody's the same."

Except me. I would kill for the chance to be the same – the same ordinary shape with an ordinary back and an ordinary family and an ordinary life.

Jay grumbled on. "And we're all expected to carry on our family's business."

"I didn't carry on my family's business."

"Maybe you should've. It sounds lucrative."

"Oh, don't take any notice of Jess," I said. "The mythical Hawn Fortune is an old rumour."

It had been dispiriting, though, to hear it resurrected. I'd thought it forgotten. If Ira had stashed away any riches, age and barley wine must have clouded all memory of its location by now. Otherwise, it would be swelling Sandy's coffers at the Barley Mow.

"Shiel knows there's nowhere to hide a treasure in our tiny cottage."

"What would you do if you found one, though?"

What indeed? With a fortune I wouldn't need to distract attention from my differences. A fortune tends to change people's attitudes towards the fortunate.

But no fortune could buy what I wanted. "Unlike some, I'm not in the habit of dreaming impossible dreams." It was too late now to hide the bitterness in my voice. "What are *you* looking for, Jay?"

"If I knew that, maybe I'd know where to look." A one-sided shrug admitted this was irrational, but that was how it was.

I could make light of it again and continue as we were. But I was weary of making light and unhappy as we were.

Friends and family saw us as a couple, but whatever future we might have together hadn't been discussed between us. Now I didn't dare initiate the conversation for fear of it becoming awkward. Jay wasn't good at saying no.

Jay

The air between us bristled with things unsaid. I suppose I assumed we'd eventually settle together... but, please, not yet.

We tend not to study the faces of people we live with. They're just there, like the furniture, and you know what they look like.

I knew that shaggy chestnut hair hid a handsome face that at least two of our school friends would have been happy to see on their pillow each morning. Both were now settled with partners from the village.

I used to wonder if some of Rob's asymmetry was deliberate, like the single earring. Then I'd remember the curving babe in the cradle. Over the years, the occasional limp and uneven shoulders were more than made up for by a wicked sense of humour, and that warm, crooked smile.

Robin wasn't smiling now.

Think about it later.

Keep talking.

"Imagine though. What would you do with all that money? Would you give up teaching?"

Brown eyes reproached me, like a beaten dog.

"Why harbour impossible dreams, Jay? Anyway, I enjoy teaching. Most of the time. Especially now I have an apprentice. I used to worry my kink might frighten the little ones, but by the time they come up from Ty's class, they're used to me."

Robin was always the one to smooth things over, restrain my excesses and make good my omissions. We would be alright again by morning, irritations forgotten. I prattled on to keep the silence at bay.

"I like tarlings in small doses, but I couldn't work with them all day like you and Ty. I'm fond of Cris and Elm's sprogs, of course. I like them even better now they wake up on the other side of the house. Brook says it's different when they're your own."

"You'd think so, wouldn't you?" Rob's head shook. "Some parents seem to see their children as part of the livestock. They don't know their own at all. Sometimes I wonder if we're discussing a different sibling, or if I've muddled up the families."

Fern barked a welcome on hearing our voices. She was silenced by a human growl.

The door was bolted, but there was no need to knock since Ira was waiting up for us. The door creaked open accompanied by mutterings. (Did we realise it was the middle of the night?) Rheumy eyes glowered, cursing me with shielfire and tarnation.

It was almost reassuring.

Some things could be relied on not to change.

Rob threw me a parting lip-twitch as I bade them good night and beat a swift retreat. A bat flew out of the eaves as I left, as if it didn't want to hang around there either.

Setting Out – Again

Robin

School was closed for the morning, but I decided to go in anyway, to escape the muttering at home. I wore my new silver sunray earring and planned to walk directly to the market square after preparing for the afternoon lessons. It would calm me to keep busy.

The door to the schoolroom was unlocked. I was sure I locked up properly yesterday. Perhaps Ty had come in early too. I called, but nobody answered.

The box felt light as I lifted it. The lock had been forced. My knife was gone, and a salve I kept for stings and grazes. I should have taken the knife home with me, but I left it here because I knew I'd need to finish the quills today.

I searched the classroom. Nothing spoke to me of who had been there, or how they had entered. I searched until I heard Ira yowling from the cottage door. I could do no more here. If we were late to the square, the wagons would be gone.

In the market square, the village had turned out to see off the convoy. The sun chose to grace the occasion, and the few fluffy clouds obliged by keeping their distance. The morning air was laced with malt and barley – libations to the shiel, of course, to invite their blessing.

I bought two beakers of cider from Sandy's stall set up outside the Barley Mow. I had no plans to buy another, and Ira had no pennies. I'd learned not to leave money lying around. It would be gone when I returned, as would Ira, to be retrieved from the Barley Mow with the help of the Cutlers.

Kip waved to us from the roadside where the wagons waited. Mikki lay under the new one, showing off Charley's springs to a Fletcher relation while Jay held forth to a group of bystanders.

Kip was a sympathetic ear. "I think the thief must have been a tarling," I said. "One of them has been taking things from class."

Kip said, "A deliberate break-in's a good deal more serious than pupils helping themselves to things lying around."

"But I think an adult wouldn't take trouble to break into a schoolroom. Whoever it is, they've covered their tracks well."

Jay's audience moved on, having exhausted the topic of Mikki's sprung wagon. Kip wanted to know if Mikki would be paying commission on sales, and I recalled Jay's reservations at the party.

"You didn't sound so keen last night."

I read a glimmer of relief behind Jay's chuckle. Equilibrium seemed to be restored. Conversation today would be constrained by the presence of Kip and Ira (where was Ira?) and our next meeting was three whole weeks away.

"I'm practising my sales patter. I'll be selling fish to the Seagen next week, just you see."

I said, "Maybe next time I'll be able to," which earned me an uncertain flicker, and Jay turned to Kip.

"You'll need to keep an eye on that long streak of insolence, Fin Hartwood, and the dumpy one, Cay, when they walk through our yard. Make sure they keep walking."

"For goodness' sake! What on earth would they want from our yard?"

Jay shrugged. "Well, they were here this morning, skulking around the wagons. After they'd gone, Sandy found money was missing."

Ira was no longer with us.

I searched the crowd and followed a trail of puzzled faces, looking for drinks they had set down a moment ago. Across the square, I spotted the crumpled hat. That cider was lasting a remarkably long time. I made my way over for a closer look.

"That's a good trick, Ira. You never showed me that one when you were teaching me salves and potions. A spell to turn cider into barley wine and double its volume. The villagers would be interested in that one. Shall we share it with them?"

Ira threw me a sour glance before nodding across the square to where wagons were moving out.

"You'll be missing your fond farewell."

Jay had mounted beside Mikki and taken the reins. They usually kept a fair distance between wagons, but Jay urged on the horses, only turning to wave as the wagon left the square, its spare horse trotting briskly behind.

When we reached the roadside, the Cutler wagon, driven by an apprentice of Mikki's, was heading out. Kip's eyes seemed thoughtful as they followed the carts.

"That was sudden." A long-fingered hand, much like Jay's, rested on my shoulder as if in sympathy.

I was glad Kip no longer read my thoughts. I tried to keep the disappointment from my face and ignore the hollowness below my ribs.

"I think I'll go into school and prepare for the afternoon." I studied Ira. "Are you in a fit condition to take yourself home?"

Ira's answering glare would wither ivy. With a departing grumble about ungrateful offspring, Ira stomped towards the Barley Mow with hardly a stagger. Sandy wouldn't be handing out free drinks, so I thought it safe to leave.

Jay

I wasn't far outside Fendle when I remembered I'd not loaded the box of Elm's hunting knives. After Fin's interest yesterday, I'd thought that box would be safer locked in the forge than sitting in a covered wagon overnight. With everything else on my mind, I'd forgotten about it this morning.

I took our wagon back to Fendle, and the apprentices got to travel in comfort with Mikki.

The square was emptying when I drove back again, although there were jokers enough to inform me I was going the wrong way. Sandy was packing up the beer stall, and Ira was lumbering unsteadily out of the square in the direction of home.

I suffered some ribbing in the workshop too when I arrived.

"Lost?" said Elm.

"Very funny. It's because of you I'm here, actually."

"Should I be flattered?"

"I've come to save you from temptation. The temptation to lynch me when I come back without selling any of your knives because I left them behind."

"That's a temptation I'd find difficult to resist."

Elm was a Tarn of few words, but adept as Kip with calculations. Both would have made sure I knew how much profit I'd forgone had I not returned for them.

Kip's voice came from my workbench. "For goodness' sake, Jay. Is that what's in this box I'm about to open?"

"That's the one; I'll load it on."

I almost fell over my feet in my hurry to retrieve the box, but Brook was closer and brought it out to the wagon.

As I secured it, Kip joined us to ask if Rob and I'd had a disagreement.

I wouldn't call it a disagreement, so I could deny it in all honesty. Kip seems to tune into my thoughts sometimes as if I were still a tarling.

I relaxed when the box was safe on the wagon with its cover intact. I'd never hear the end of it if anyone'd spotted that flaming list on top of the knives.

Mercifully, the jokers had gone, and the tarlings were all in school when I got away again. Only Sandy still sat there, sipping at an ale and watching the pigeons clear the crumbs from the market square.

I made good time after that. Tarn is a flat land and the first day out is easy on the horses. The view's not as picturesque as Wendale's swooping hills and valleys. Most of our scenery is sky. The Seagen wax lyrical about the horizon out at sea being a complete circle around you. But that's not so amazing. It's the same when you stand in the middle of Tarn's fields. There, the horizon's an unbroken line whichever way you turn, apart from a hiccup or two from the odd tree in the distance – not enough to spoil the effect. And we have an added advantage. There's little chance of drowning in Tarn.

I met the Hunsfen convoy on the way and we arrived together at the field behind the Copper Kettle in Weffen, where we always make camp the first night. Mikki came to help unhitch the horse, and that's when I discovered my knife was gone.

Its sheath was unfastened. I can't have hooked it properly this morning and the knife must have fallen out. I kept searching long after I knew it wasn't on the wagon, as if it would appear if I looked hard enough.

With any luck, the knife will have dropped near the forge where someone would recognise it and hold it for me. That knife had been my first adult achievement. I'd been proud of it then, and I still treasured it.

I told myself I could mourn and fret about it for the next couple of weeks, or I could put it out of my mind, and hope that someone would find and keep it for me. Whether I worried or trusted wouldn't affect the outcome, so I resolved to forget about it until I was home.

If the worst happened, after all, I could make another.

Robin

Jess and Taz sat at the back of the room, radiating disapproval as the tarlings nudged each other and made faces. Every question I asked prompted giggles instead of answers. After a frustrating half-hour, I was relieved when the Minstrers moved on to Ty's class for the rest of the afternoon.

I took longer than usual locking up, but the Minstrers still stood at the school gate, giving Ty the benefit of their advice as I passed. I managed to slip away unaccosted while Ty hovered, small and round, blinking owlishly in search of a conversational gap to swoop a goodbye into.

Buoyed by my escape, I strove to feel positive as I walked home, enjoying the still-warm autumn sun on my face and the hint of bonfires in the air.

Fern limped out to greet me. Her greeting was hesitant, not her usual happy bounce. Her tail wagged uncertainly. Something was wrong. Why was the door open?

Ira's hat lay on the ground outside. I picked it up and pushed the door wider. The hinges protested, and I shivered, but not because of the unlit fire, not even laid yet. A buzzing fly rose from our uncleared breakfast plates and settled again.

Where was Ira? The door was always closed when I got home whatever the weather. Sometimes it was even bolted shut and I had to shout to be let in.

I lit a lamp, and pots hanging over the fireplace threw back the light. I called out, not that I couldn't see the whole cottage from where I stood. So I went to the door to call again.

Outside the school, Ty had flown, and the Minstrers were strolling this way. No Ira.

I turned to scan our sparsely furnished room for an explanation to reassure me. Instead, something on the floor flashed, "Over here!"

It was a shining handle etched with a pattern that caught the light – the handle of a knife.

I watched my hand pick it up and hold it to the light, then flinch and drop it on the table. Something had crusted on the blade, as blood does when it dries.

With the uncanny ability of busybodies to sense when they're not wanted, Taz and Jess had reached the cottage. They may have heard the clatter of the knife, or I may have cried out. Something prompted them to look through the door.

It was, of course, Jess who recognised the knife as Jay's

Day Two, Jay

After our first night out, we were up with the lark.

Only, it wasn't a lark, according to Mikki, when they came to rouse me. The bird singing its heart out from the roof of the Copper Kettle's stables seemed too tiny for the glorious song that filled the stable yard. I had to watch its beak to make sure I had the right warbler.

We were harnessed up and on our way long before Rob would be opening up at school. A shadow overhung the thought of Rob, but I remembered my resolve to set Fendle matters aside until I could do something about them. If anything needed to be done.

The morning smelled of horse and harness. All Rob's musks and spices could never compete with the scents of a journey. The road we travelled bordered Wendale and already the landscape was changing. Shadows of scudding clouds swept across the usual autumn patchwork of yellow harvested stubble, brown turned fields, and green meadows. But here, the patchwork was spread over rolling hills and dipped into valleys where the rivers ran faster than Tarn's.

Wenn's woodland smelled different too, and there was more of it. Wild boar had spread from the Shade Forest to Wendale's shademost woods, but none had been sighted this far noonward. Hunting parties went out from the fairs for those with a fancy to hunt boar, but it was a risky business. Mikki's partner died on a boar hunt years ago, before I started working the fairs. Since then, Mikki only hunted rabbits and ground-birds.

The new cart was like linen after sacking; smooth and comfortable. Mikki had begun to look out for ruts and bumps to aim it at, but the rains had been well-spaced this autumn and roads were still firm. The cart showed no signs of falling apart, but I didn't think we should look for trouble and said so.

Mikki dismissed my protests. "You should show more faith in your cousin and me. When have our wagons ever let you down?"

"There's a first time for everything. Although, I'll grant you, this one's a different beast from the old boneshaker I drove yesterday. I bet young Danni notices the difference tonight."

"I expect young Danni'll be far too busy to notice any aches and pains." Mikki gave a chuckle.

Danni had enjoyed the company of a young Tarn from Hunsfen yesterday evening and by the end of the usual first-night singalong both had disappeared. This morning, a cheer had gone up from the Hunsfen wagons, followed by a similar salute from Fendle's travellers when Danni appeared.

They weren't the only missing youngsters who joined their wagons looking sheepish or pleased with themselves. More seasoned travellers were less likely to be sharing a bedroll so close to home unless their partner had come with them. A few might have reunions planned at the fair's ground, with a Wenn or Llann, or one of the coastal clans – the dark, rugged Seagen differed again from our tall, fair-haired Marin neighbours. They were all fascinating to this sparrow-brown earthbound Tarn.

I wished Danni well. "We've all been there."

I ignored the smile that creased Mikki's face and asked, "Are you meeting up with anyone in High Wenn?"

"Oh no, not me. I take each fair as it comes, no regrets, no comebacks. Hawk's my bedroll buddy. He makes a good footwarmer."

Hawk was Mikki's hound. In fact, Mikki didn't want for admirers, being still attractive and fit in a mature sort of way. Hawk would more likely be keeping watch than warming the bedroll.

"How come you're not getting wider as you get older, like my parents? Cris is already looking more like Brook every year."

"What's wrong with looking like Brook, then?" Mikki flung me a disapproving frown. "I keep busy and cook for just me. You don't eat so much when you're not feeding someone else as well. Someone told me once that debts and waistlines are easier to grow than they are to shrink."

I wondered who that had been, but not enough to ask. "Have you never wanted to settle again?"

"I'm not sure I'd fancy anyone who's old as I am."

"You're not crumbling yet, old love. How old are you, anyway?"

Mikki lifted the straw hat and scratched where the brim had been.

"I suppose I must be fortysomething; we'd not long settled when you were born." The hat rested again on unruly hair that gleamed whiter than a goat's pelt.

"Well, I hope I look as good when I get to forty." It was too far ahead to imagine. "Were you happy being settled?" I'd never ventured to raise the subject before.

"Very."

"Yet you didn't want to try it again, after Ches?"

"It wasn't a conscious decision. It just never came up."

"Nobody who measured up then?"

"If you mean measure up to Ches, I'm not looking to. You can't shoe-horn someone into somebody else's boots. Not that Ches was perfect. But neither was I."

Mikki threw me a grin. "I am now, of course."

"How do you decide, though, who to settle with for the rest of your life? There might be someone else you haven't met yet."

"I reckon you'll know when you stop looking." Mikki's drawl sharpened. "It's a nice, romantic notion that you've got a soulmate out there somewhere, but if that's how it works, they might've been born on the other side of the counties, and you'll never meet 'em. Then there'd be fewer 'lings born, and we'd be ghost counties again, like after the Sickness."

"But if you're going to spend the rest of your life together, you have to be sure, don't you?"

"You need more time to get to know Robbie, is that it?"

I glanced across at Mikki, whose gaze was fixed on the road ahead.

"Course not."

It was other people I wanted time to get to know. But I didn't feel I could say that.

And the adviser I usually shared my problems with was the one person I couldn't talk to about this. Laughter drifted forward from the apprentices in the cart behind us.

"I don't know. Maybe I'm not ready yet to be stuck in Fendle with a litter of tarlings and nothing to look forward to."

The wheels rolled a couple of turns.

"Rob wants more, and I don't know what to do about it."

Mikki's eyes were still on the road ahead. "What do you want to do about it?"

"I want us to stay the way we are."

"Things don't stay the way they are. People grow up." Another roll of the wheels. "Most people."

Mikki's sharp eyes turned to me with a frown between them. "It would be better to be up front about it and put some distance between you, then. You know Robbie's grown up worshipping your shadow?"

"Well, younger sibs do that, don't they? And we're almost family."

"You get on that well with Cris, then?"

"That's different. Cris isn't like me."

"Neither's Robbie."

That was true. "But we like the same things, mostly."

"Is that enough, d'you think?"

I'd thought not. I thought there must be more. The trouble was, every time I pursued this elusive "more" it faded soon after I caught up with it, like the morning moon after sunrise.

"Rob hasn't had much of a life, what with the kink and the grouch to cope with." For the first time I felt a twinge of guilt. "I don't want to be responsible for mucking it up even more."

"I won't argue with that." The wheels rolled a couple more turns. "Feeling sorry for someone isn't the best of reasons to settle with 'em for the rest of your lives."

Wasn't that what I wanted to hear?

"I know. Rob deserves better than that."

Mikki nodded again, conclusively. "Robbie's a good kid. It's a shame."

What was? The kink? Or Rob's misplaced affection for me?

I didn't ask. We drove on in companionable silence as clouds thickened in the sky to match those now gathering over my thoughts.

Most of our school friends had settled now with tarlings of their own.

The looming cloud mass darkened, and the air felt damp.

Rob had gently rebuffed other romantic advances in the years since school. I suppose that was my fault, too.

A freshening breeze made me shiver, and my attention returned to the clouds above. With luck, it might not rain until we'd made camp.

Day Two, Robin

All night I listened for a footstep but heard only the cries of hunting animals. My chest was a void where trapped birds fluttered. I swung between one worry and another.

Ira had been gone all night and was old.

Jess had Jay's knife and a malicious imagination.

Jess was quick to pounce on the knife yesterday, sniffing at the stain like a bloodhound, and then nodding with satisfaction.

But Ira was with me when Jay left Fendle. Someone else must have left the knife at our cottage.

Ira's walking stick was missing too, so we'd headed for the Barley Mow, stopping at the forge to pick up Cris and Elm in case any carrying was required. That was where we learned of the box that had been forgotten. Jay came back for it, leaving again around midday.

Jess lapped up this news.

Of course, Ira wasn't at the Barley Mow and hadn't been seen since leaving Sandy in the market square that morning. Some of the inn's customers set out to search, but it was getting dark by then.

Jess insisted the knife must go with them to Tarfen, so both Minstrers came back with me to the cottage.

Ira still wasn't there.

Jess lit all the lanterns and carried one into every corner, searching under furniture, rifling through Ira's linen trunk and even among our bedclothes, hoping to find heaven knows what. Another weapon, perhaps? Or a puddle of blood.

But there was no pool of blood, only a smear where the blade had rested on the flagstone.

I found rag to wrap the knife while Jess snooped around again, as if disappointed there wasn't more of the cottage to search.

I gave up hope of sleep that night. When a crack of light appeared between window shutters, I watched it brighten with the dawn.

All night, my mind had sought Jay's, unable to connect. Yet again, I told myself it was time to give up on this unreliable bond.

The ballads tell of old times when people could properly connect at a distance if they chose and hear the other's thoughts as if they were words. How had we lost this ability? Had thoughts been blocked too often, as Jay blocked ours? Had they withered from misuse until linked minds could now share only each other's feelings? I could do little more than send Jay my fear and hope that would be warning enough.

But it seemed I couldn't do that either.

I gave up trying and reached for the jug to fill the kettle. The jug was as empty as my channel to Jay. I threw it at the wall in frustration, and Fern took off through her escape hatch. She had an opening at the back of the cottage with a weighted sack hung as a flap to keep out draughts. I had fenced an area outside with a barrier low enough for me to step over. Fern couldn't jump it with her weak leg.

The jug was fortunately a metal one from the Cutlers. As I bent to retrieve it, I was angry with the world, but especially with Jay. And with Ira, who was probably sleeping it off in a ditch somewhere.

So I walked the ditches around our nearest fields. Then I searched the trees along the lane. Where next? Ira wouldn't willingly walk far unless there was a drink in it. My head throbbed through lack of sleep and the constant, futile search for Jay.

Kip and Cris arrived as I was dithering in the lane. Kip had offered to teach my class today.

They said I should wait at the cottage in case Ira turned up. They probably thought I would slow the searchers, but I did see the sense of it. Cris left with the villagers who arrived to help. They went to search along Ira's path from the market square, and Kip stayed with me until school opened. I felt I should be doing more.

Not long after Kip left, Taz and Jess arrived. They were about to leave for Tarfen to deliver Jay's knife to the office of the Watchguards. Jess's air of self-importance challenged my civility.

"You're fishing in the wrong pond, Administrator Giltin. It's true they didn't get on, but Jay had no reason to harm Ira."

"Hmph. Money's always reason enough." Jess's pitying look was a silent insult. "There are plenty still wondering what happened to the profits Sal left from such a thriving business. I don't see remains of it here." Of course! That was the reason for all the snooping last night.

"Unless the Cutlers spent it. Hmph."

My overstretched control threatened to snap. "I hope you're not suggesting the Cutlers took Ira's money?"

"No. No, of course…. Harrumph. I'd expect them to have a bit more to show for it if they had. You may not be aware that the Cutlers are in debt for a substantial amount of money."

How did Jess know that? Brook guarded that information like the recipe for a secret potion. No-one outside the family knew of it.

"I am aware they've taken a loan. Repayment is in hand. There isn't a problem. You're probably not aware that we were living on the Cutlers' charity until Administrator Fletcher offered me the school. Ira drank away any money Sal left years ago. Furthermore, as an Administrator of the Tarn Lower Assembly, I would have thought you should be above perpetuating unfounded rumours!"

Taz, at least, had the grace to look embarrassed.

"Robin, I know you're worried for Jay as well…" Word of Ira's disappearance had spread last night. Every village has its feral side with bullies eager for a witch-hunt and disinclined to spare the witch. "I'll be speaking to the Minstrer in charge of the Watchguards, either this afternoon or first thing tomorrow. If it seems advisable, Watchguards can meet the wagons before they reach Fendle and take Jay to somewhere safe in Tarfen."

"Somewhere safe" was, no doubt, a tactful euphemism. If it was meant to reassure me, it failed miserably by confirming that Taz thought someone might take Jess's grotesque suspicions seriously.

And where was the miserable old grouch causing all this trouble?

If I were honest, the absence of Ira was no burden. The absence of information, on the other hand – not knowing where to look, or why, or even what we were looking for – kept me swinging between anger and anxiety.

Should I be doing more? And, if so, what?

Whatever our differences, that miserable old grouch was the only family I had.

The Administrators left. The searchers returned empty-handed. Some had work waiting for them; others were enjoying the drama and went for lunch at the Barley Mow. As they left the cottage, the Hartwoods were expanding on the chances of being murdered in their beds.

"If Ira had been murdered in bed, at least we'd know where to look for a body."

Brook's smile was sympathetic. "Where else should we look, Robin?" I had been asking myself that all morning. "Might someone have taken Ira?"

"Why would anyone want to?"

That resurrected rumour of hidden wealth hovered in the background.

They left to resume the search, but I doubted many would be persuaded away from the warmth of the inn now. They expected to find a body, and where was the urgency in that? Most had no care to find a living Ira, who they'd long suspected of sorcery or worse.

But they would enjoy hounding Jay, given scent of a cause.

Kip came after school and told me how the day had gone. It was a surreal fragment of normality.

"I'm grateful Kip. I know you're busy."

"Oh, for goodness' sake... we're in no need of new designs at the moment, and I can do the bookkeeping in my sleep now. Today was like snuggling into a comfortable old coat I'd forgotten I had. I'm available for as long as you want me."

"Thanks, Kip."

I knew, though, that this wasn't entirely true. Kip might not be working the metal, but the forge would need every pair of hands to help with the new tavern's order. I couldn't face work while Ira was missing and Jay was under suspicion.

Kip's eyes on my bitten finger-ends prompted me to turn and fill the kettle. "I'm glad the children didn't play you up." *And put you off.*

"They've been strangely quiet, even the ones I expected trouble from." Concerned grey eyes probed mine. "How have you been, Robin? Why don't you come home with me? Join us for dinner. I don't think you should be sitting here on your own."

No expectation of Ira returning now. The evening stretched ahead. The warm familiarity of Jay's family beckoned.

"Thank you, I'd like that. Although I won't be very good company."

"You don't have to be. You're family."

My spirits dropped whenever Jay said that, but from Kip, it was welcome.

The pups were weaned now, but I watched them feed and made sure Fern could get out of her door if she needed to.

"The pups will soon be big enough to follow her over the skirting. I doubt they'll grow big enough to jump the fence."

"Are they getting enough food?"

"I think so." I rolled one over and rubbed his fat little belly.

"Yes, I see what you mean."

His legs scrabbled the air in delight and others came to investigate.

As I locked the cottage door, Kip's eyes were creased in thought. "I wonder how Marmalade would take to a puppy?"

On the walk to the forge, I asked, "How does Jess know about the loan?"

"That's where it came from. Jess's interest rates are lower than Tarfen moneylenders, as long as we pay it back on time."

I shivered. Rain was coming in; I could smell it in the air.

Day Five, Jay

We reached High Wenn later than we'd planned. The rain slowed us, and each day's journey stretched longer to compensate. As we crossed the bridge by the Green Man, the heavens relented, and the rain held off long enough for us to stable the horses and make camp. Then the clouds tipped again.

The Llann and Seagen had already arrived, so the best pitches were taken. We settled for a spot that was nearer to the tavern and the river than we'd have liked, but if the weather didn't improve we'd have more than noise and insects to worry about. We ate under cover in the wagon.

Glyn, my Llann companion from spring's fair, defied the rain to come and greet us with partner in tow. They appeared at the wagon's end and Glyn began hasty introductions before I said anything incriminating. Meanwhile, those dark oval eyes signalled a warning, in case I'd forgotten they'd be here together.

I hadn't forgotten.

They came in out of the rain, pushing their hoods back from identical ragged haircuts. Water trailed down their backs onto the wagon's boards.

"When I saw you pull in, I thought we should drop by on our way to the tavern, like. Will you be coming over later?"

"Probably not tonight."

We'd already decided to give it a miss that night. We were drained from another long, wet day and our scurry to make camp between downpours. Now we were dry, we didn't fancy getting wet again.

Bursts of laughter and good-natured shouting came from the tavern, and when I raised the flap of the wagon to look, people were struggling to get through the door because of the crush inside. Mikki looked over my shoulder.

"I'm surprised they haven't put up the shelters outside yet."

"It hasn't stopped raining long enough to get them up. The Seagen are inside with a foreigner; that's why it's so busy, like. They brought someone with them who claims to come from the other side of the Shade Forest."

Glyn might as well have said they'd brought one of the shiel with them.

The Shade Forest was home to wolves and wild boar and big feral cats. As far as anyone knew, it might stretch on to the end of the world. The few brave souls who'd tried to find out hadn't been seen again.

I was tempted to go with Glyn and Hazen to the Green Man, but another peek through the rain dissuaded me. It was unlikely we'd get anywhere near the fire once we got there. Mikki wished them good luck as they raised their hoods, and we watched their dash to the tavern.

Tomorrow would be a better night for the Green Man on the evening before the fair opened. The last of the merchants will have arrived, and we'd be looking to meet up with old friends and make new ones. We'd meet this foreigner soon enough.

Robin

For two days it rained, as if the sky was shedding the tears I couldn't. We waited, not knowing what else to do. I felt useless, waiting in the cottage, but quailed at the thought of work. I still couldn't reach Jay.

If I did make contact, what could I send but my worry? Jay was always telling me I worried too much.

If only I could follow the convoy… But how? I had ridden for short distances but always suffered afterwards. The jogging hurt my back. Knowing that, who would lend me their horse? And how would I know which way to go when tracks separated? Not all roads were signposted.

I'd often shared my thoughts with Fern in whispers when Ira was asleep. She was a good listener. Now I talked as I made the tea or cleared the grate. I doubt I always made sense, but Fern didn't mind. Anyone within hearing might think I was losing my mind, talking to myself.

Kip came every day after school to update me on the day's learning.

I tried to sound interested. "I am glad they're still cooperating. The ones who are leaving often lose interest around now and it unsettles the rest of the class."

Kip nodded as I put the teapot on the table and went back for cups.

"Yes, I used to save more interesting lessons for the last weeks of term. So this afternoon we've been looking at arrows – metals, weight, what to look for in a good tip… that sort of thing."

"That's a good idea." I sat and poured our tea. "I'm sure Fin knows better, though, and tells you when you're wrong." The Hartwoods were hunters.

"I'd expected that too," said Kip. "I was quite prepared to bow to the expert and hand the class over to Fin if it kept things moving, but it's been uncommonly quiet in that corner." Kips's hands cradled the warm cup. (*Should I stoke the stove?*) "I've hardly heard a squeak out of the usual troublemakers. Something's ruffled their feathers."

The grey eyes were thoughtful as Kip sipped the hot tea. "Cay's out of favour with Fin for some reason."

"Lovers' tiff?" I wondered aloud. "I didn't expect that unholy alliance to last as long as it has. I doubt Fin would tolerate Cay so well if they hadn't lived next door to each other all their lives." Cay wasn't the sharpest knife on the rack, while Fin didn't miss a thing behind that shield of indifference. "It must be irritating sometimes to have Cay always trailing behind like a needy chick."

Did I irritate Jay?

Kip's voice followed me as I fed the stove. "I'm going to ask the Fletchers if I can bring the class to their workshop for some practical tips on shafts, nocks, fletching…"

"I'm sure Taz would approve."

"Did you know Taz is back?" Now Kip had my full attention. "Brook came to say they'd be out hunting by the time I get home. Elm went to the Fletchers to barter some new tips for more arrows, and Taz arrived with a younger Minstrer who's going to be staying with them."

"Come to find what happened to Ira."

"That's what I thought. Elm didn't ask."

I registered what Kip had said before. "Who's looking after the tarlings then, if they're all out hunting?"

"Cris didn't go this time and is feeding them as we speak."

"Then why don't you stay and eat with me? Fern and I would be glad of your company."

I didn't want to be alone just yet to think about "what ifs". I wanted to fill every minute until something started happening. It was a relief to know it would start happening soon.

That was before I met Eden Thatcher.

Day Six, Meetings

Jay

At last, the rain had stopped.

Danni and Kyl, the apprentices, helped me rig two sturdy shelters that would keep off rain and withstand the wind, which was moderate by Tarn standards. The Green Man stood beside a river, which provided our water, and the site was sheltered, in a valley with trees along one side of the field.

Wenn fairs had changed over the years. Now most of the bidding was for goods to be delivered direct to the buyer's village. Mikki brought the new cart to attract orders, not to sell it off.

Still, there was cash profit to be had from the stalls. People came to fairs in a mood to spend money. Stallholders looked for something to take home for the 'lings, or a keepsake to give to a bedroll buddy.

Our shelters held trestles to display our wares and those of our Wysmith, Locke and Naismith cousins from neighbouring villages. The covered wagons served as offices for discussing discounts and delivery arrangements. I kept some of my jewellery with me – the cheaper sets, which might sell for a few coins or be bartered for goods on the other stalls. My silver would come out tomorrow, when the fair began properly and the wealthy townsfolk from High Wenn, or further afield, came looking for trinkets.

The field buzzed with activity. From time to time, the sun emerged to dry the ground and sparkle on the river. Clouds parted as we stopped for food. We basked in gentle sunlight and talked about ways to attract custom to our stalls while Mikki went for ale. Danni always thought up new ideas for displaying stock and rearranging as it sold.

By the time the ale arrived, the clouds had closed ranks again. We presented our beakers for Mikki to fill.

"There's a good atmosphere in the tavern. Even the Llann aren't complaining about anything yet."

The atmosphere outside concerned me more. "We could do with a good Tarn blow to chase these clouds away."

Danni peered across the field towards the burst of laughter. "There's a fair amount of merriment out here as well."

Approaching us was the most gorgeous creature I'd ever seen, accompanied by a motley group hanging on every word. The orator was taller than any of them and leaner than most. A musical voice carried across the distance between us, and I recognised the extravagant tones of a born storyteller.

That should have been my first warning.

But I was already dazzled. As the group drew near, the clear blue of the speaker's eyes stood out against honey-coloured skin. Raven-dark hair curled into the back of their neck, framing small, delicate ears. The ears weren't actually pointed, but it would hardly have surprised me if they were – like a creature from another world.

Which I suppose Storm was, in a manner of speaking.

Next moment the laughing eyes met mine and Storm smiled, nodding a greeting, as if we had met before, in a previous life.

Mikki grunted and turned away. "That one's trouble."

Robin

Fern's bark was quickly followed by a knock at the door.

I opened it, to find Taz on my doorstep, standing beside a Tarn who resembled a string bean – as would most people next to Taz. Taller than me (everyone's taller than me), taller than Jay and holding a leather satchel, this must be the Minstrer from Tarfen we were waiting for.

Fern came to greet them, followed by her pups, who now had the run of the place. They would tumble out after Fern to her fenced-off run and were house-training themselves. Taz evaded the pups and the newcomer ignored them. I told Fern to go in her bed and the pups trailed after her.

"Robin, this is Eden Thatcher, the Administrator in charge of the Watchguards. That's a new Administration office to look into things that… hmm… need looking into."

The official tone faltered, before resuming with confidence, "Things like people going missing and complaints of violence or wrongdoing… that sort of thing."

Eden Thatcher acknowledged the introduction with a nod and a compression of thin lips which might have been meant as a smile.

"Come in. Sit down." I turned a fireside chair to join the two at the table. "Can I get you a drink? Tea?

Gooseberry wine?" – trying desperately to remember where I'd last hidden it.

"Thank you, water will be fine. If you have any."

Clearly, the offer of gooseberry wine marked me as a habitual drunkard. Fortunately, a jug of water waited by the sink, boiled this morning and well cooled. Ira's apothecary habits came in useful sometimes.

Taz declined. "Nothing for me. Thank you, Robin. I have to get on. Administrator chores, you know, while I'm in the village." (Condescending smile towards me.) "I'm just here to introduce Eden and help out with any local knowledge." (Ingratiating smile to Eden.) "So, I'll leave you to it." And with a final untargeted beam, Taz swept out.

I poured two cups of water as Eden settled at the table and opened the bag.

This Minstrer was younger than I'd expected an Administrator to be. Younger than Kip. Nose a bit hawkish... otherwise angular features with no expression at all. The fine, light brown hair tucked behind neat ears glowed where summer had lightened it. I took the chair opposite.

On the table two pens had appeared, as well as paper and a small flask of ink from which the stopper was being removed by well-manicured hands with nails polished to a shine.

"I understand this must be upsetting for you." Eden blinked. "I have to ask about the day Ira went missing. You understand, I've only heard third-hand accounts so far."

And Jess's lurid theories. I understood only too well.

Once again, I relived the events of that morning and of the evening. I recounted what Ira would do on a typical day, what I would do on a typical day, what I had done that afternoon, what Ira had probably done, what Fern might have done (!) and then we came to the knife. Long fingers unwrapped the bundle of rag taken from a drawstring bag. The rusty stain was still on the blade.

"Do you recognise this?"

"Of course. It's Jay's. I've no idea why it was here. I don't know if that's blood on the blade either, but Taz will confirm there was none on the floor."

I hoped my voice sounded more confident than I felt. How could I convince this stranger of the absurdity of Jess's suspicion?

"…And whatever it is on the blade, I'm sure you'll agree there's hardly enough to suggest a mortal wound."

The only sound was the pen scratching.

"What do you think?" I despised the tremor that had crept into my voice.

"I can't think anything until I have all the information. Might the dogs have cleared up any blood on the floor?"

My growing dislike blossomed. Remote and unsmiling, Eden Thatcher gave nothing away, showed no hint of humanity and posed the next question before I'd tackled the last.

"How far would Ira be able to walk unaided?"

"Not very. I suppose to the Barley Mow. And back, with a long break in between."

I re-ran that again in my memory. Might it have sounded flippant from someone who had recently lost a parent? Literally.

"Less, of course, with a wound." That brought me back to attention. "As you've pointed out, there's nothing so far to suggest heavy blood loss, but any injury could make a difference to someone of Ira's age… Sixty, is it?"

"I'm not sure."

I should have been. I'd thought about it before, of course, but nobody seemed to know for certain. Ira didn't invite that kind of question.

"I know my parents weren't young when they settled, and there was one before me."

"And you are?"

"Twenty-one," I supplied, while my thoughts wandered again. They'd told me Ira was attractive back before Sal died, before the bitterness and the drinking…

The pen scratched.

"It's hard to imagine Ira ever being good-looking."

I had spoken aloud. Warmth rose to my cheeks. It was irrelevant. Eden had never met Ira. The pen stopped. I was being assessed – for signs of a guilty conscience, no doubt. I made my eyes meet those pale brown pebbles, but they were unreadable.

"Can you think of anyone who would want to harm Ira?"

Apart from me? "Not really. We have no neighbours and Ira rarely goes out."

Then I remembered. Eden would hear it from someone.

"There was a rumour that we had money hidden in the cottage, but I can't imagine anyone would seriously believe it."

I looked around helplessly at the comfortable chaos. Eden followed my gaze but forbore to comment.

"Yes, Taz Fletcher mentioned that. I understand the Cutlers know Ira as well as anyone?"

"We lived with them while I was growing up. And, of course, they're Jay's parents."

"Of course. And they have another…" notes were consulted. "Cris? Partner Elmer; three children." I nodded. Pale eyes blinked. "Then that's where I should go next."

The pen stopped scratching, and a cloth materialised to wipe it. This was folded carefully with the ink stain inside and another scrap produced to wrap pens and wiper.

"I hope I can help you find Ira, or at least discover what happened."

The report and knife were already in the leather bag. The ink followed, securely sealed and wrapped. "Thank you for your patience."

We stood, and a measured smile rippled the surface as Eden Thatcher looked down at me across the table.

Bony, I thought.

I led the way to the door and caught the hint of a subtle floral fragrance as I held it open. Not as nice as the ones I mixed, of course.

I wanted to say something in defence of Jay, but nothing came to mind that wouldn't sound desperate. I settled for "Goodbye," and watched the Minstrer off the premises. From behind, I noticed how the simple dove-grey tunic suit flattered the rangy body and reflected that Administrators could afford to dress well out of our taxes.

Turning, I stepped into puppy mess.

I made sure the lane was empty before I hopped outside to clean my shoe. As I went back in to clear the mess on the floor, Fern kept out of my way.

The interview had scattered the fog shrouding my wits.

Would Eden Thatcher find Ira? Did Eden, too, suspect Jay? I found myself fervently hoping that it would all turn out to be an evil scheme of Ira's who we would find somewhere, safe and cackling.

I realised it was the first time I had actively wished for the old grouch to be alive.

Day Six, The Green Man

Jay

The sky cleared, although the sun had barely time to warm the air before it sank behind the treetops. Mikki joined the locals and the older traders crowded inside the Green Man tavern. The rest of us sat around campfires set outside.

"I hear you've met our Storm, then."

"Almost." I turned at the familiar voice and looked up into Samphire's keen seafarer's eyes. Spare and ageless, Sam was a Marin from the coast nearest to Tarn and was beautiful, but firmly settled with Kel in Seacrag. Kel was another stunner, tall for a Seagan and sable-haired to Sam's flax. Like black and white swans, though I'd only seen them once together. They'd met at a Wenn fair, but now Kel came to the spring fairs and Samphire the autumn ones, subject to the demands of childbirth, while the other stayed home to mind the spratlings.

"This is our eldest, Kestrel. Come to keep an eye on me."

A spratling of maybe ten summers smiled up at this unlikely charge. Kestrel was dark like Kel, but with Samphire's piercing blue eyes. A heavy pigtail hung down the 'ling's back, in the manner of shorefolk whichever coast they hail from.

"So, what did you think of Storm, then?" Samphire prompted.

I glanced at Kestrel and thought better of voicing the first reply that came to mind. "How did you meet?"

The Seagen were basking in their second-hand celebrity. Samphire held a brimming beaker, filled by the last group who'd heard the story. They made themselves comfortable at our campfire and Sam related what must by now be a well-rehearsed tale.

"We was out fishing and a squall caught us. We was slow to drop sail and wind took en; t'were ripped afore we had en down. Two of us tried rowing, but Kel thought we'd lose the oars, so we sat tight. When wind dropped, we'd lost sight of land."

Sam paused for effect, lifting the beaker. Storytelling was thirsty work.

"When things quieted, we couldn't agree which way land was. We was drifting, but there's no benefit in rowing in wrong direction. When the cloud thinned and we could tell where sun was, we rowed dawnwards, but by then we'd drifted too far, and when we sighted land, it were all trees. We didn't want to risk the Shade Forest…"

Nobody would want to risk the Shade Forest. Sam's sups and the fire's crackle were the only sounds from our spellbound circle.

"There was nought to be done but keep land in sight and row noonwards, but we was getting fair desperate by then. We needed to rest up and try to salvage some sail to carry us home, so when we came to an inlet, we rowed in and anchored out in the middle." Sam took another sip.

Kyl and Danni were spellbound. Kestrel watched a beetle scuttle through the grass.

"Well, we re-rigged what sail were left, and we heard this hollering from mainland. Even where we was, you could tell en was in a bad way. There was nought to be done but stow sail again and row over. We was ready to leave en to it though, if we sighted trouble."

Sam's modest disclaimer drew sympathetic murmurs.

"In the end, the poor beggar swam out soon as we was close enough and it were Storm, lost in Forest while chasing horse or some such."

Samphire sounded doubtful about that. No horse was worth following into the Shade Forest.

"Been wandering with no food nigh on two days. Wanted us to head shadeward, but that weren't going to happen. We thought to be lucky if our dicky-rigged sail'd last long enough to see us home, and Kel's family fretting if we wasn't back for the spratlings."

The beaker lifted again, but its contents were gone. I sent Danni for refills.

"So, I said I'd take Storm home when we're back from the fair."

A voice behind me broke the silence.

"I didn't think there was anything shadeward of the Forest."

"Neither did none of us. But now we knows, it can't do no harm to see if there's trade to be done." Sam's eyes gleamed in the firelight.

Outside the glow of the campfires, dusk had deepened. Storm emerged from the gloom chatting to a short, thickset Llann. As they entered the firelight, I recalled Opal from a couple of years ago, only with fewer chins back then. The Llann were compact, swarthy people. Those who worked underground were ingrained with dust from the mines, and those who didn't were weatherbeaten by the mountain winds; I'd never seen a llanling to know how they started out. Underground workers liked to keep their hair cropped, to cover easily against the dust. Opal's was long, dark and oily.

They greeted us and Opal went for drinks. Storm chatted with the group around the next campfire before coming to sit by Kestrel and turning to me. "You're Jay. You're set up over there."

I didn't recall us exchanging names; Storm must have asked someone. I could feel my smile stretching towards my ears.

"You're the Tarn with the pretty armlets."

"And there was me thinking it was my baby-blue eyes."

Storm leaned closer. "They're grey."

I took an armlet off my wrist.

"Would you like one? It matches the pendant." I selected the necklet in question and took it from my neck. These were made from base metal, but had they been silver, I would have still offered them.

Kestrel's eyes were wide, and Samphire clamped down the small hand that had raised to claim my attention.

"And if Kes would like to come to our wagon tomorrow morning, I'm sure I have another sample."

Danni's eyes were nearly as wide as Kestrel's. "Are–?"

"One that might fit an arm of ten or eleven summers." I'd seen no 'lings younger than Kes with the stallholders.

Samphire was quietly amused and leaned to whisper in my ear. "You know Kes already made friends with innkeeper's young 'uns."

I looked into Sam's eyes to see if this was a joke.

"I'll have a quiet word when I'm putting en to bed. I thank you for that. You didn't have to."

I shrugged. I probably would have found something for Kestrel anyway, less publicly. Storm had meanwhile fastened the pendant's necklet and was admiring the armlet, which now encircled a slender, tanned wrist. I claimed my payment.

"So where are you from, exactly?"

"From Westhaven. In Scarth. I'm Storm, by the way. Storm Heron."

I was treated to a full-on, fifty-candle, daybreak of a smile. I grinned back like an idiot.

"Jay Cutler. From Tarn."

"Now there's another place I've not heard of. There we were thinkin there was nothing at all past the Border Forest." ("That's what Scarthers call the Shade Forest," whispered Kes) "–And now they're tellin me there's a whole world over here as well. How far's Tarn then?"

"You're nearly there. We're the next county dawnwards. After Tarn, there's just Marsea along the coast. Noonward of us is wasteland. There's only scrub there. Beyond the scrub, they say it's just black earth where not even moss grows, but nobody knows anyone who's been to see."

We exchanged backgrounds. Storm's family bred horses. More people came and groups merged, jostling us closer. Then the singing started up. Some nudging went on with heads nodding in Kestrel's direction, so our group started up *Green Grow the Rushes* to drown out the others.

Storm started to sing along but faltered at the second verse and stopped to listen. After that, those clear, ringing tones joined in toward the end of each verse, coming in earlier each time as more lines became familiar.

When it was finished, Storm said, "We've different words for that one in Scarth. Although yours makes more sense. Sort of."

Someone asked, "What words do you sing then?"

Storm sang us a full verse.

I'll sing you twelve songs; Green grow the rushes-o.
What are your twelve songs?
Twelve for the twelve lost portals;
Eleven for the eleven that went to heaven, and
Ten for the ten commandments;
Nine for the nine bright shiners;
Eight for the eight hill-rainers;
Seven for the seven stars in the sky, and
Six for the six brown stalkers;
Five for the cymbals at your door, and
Four for the gods' spell-makers.
Three, three, the ri-i-i-ivals.
Two, two, the lily-white flowers, cloth-ed all in green-o.
One is one and all alone and ever more shall be so.

There was a moment's silence until someone said, "Yer right, it dun't make sense. It dun even rhyme! Nice voice though."

"Come on Kes Fisher. Time for your bed, I reckon."

Samphire took Kestrel off to bed, and we closed the gap between us.

Since Kes was still in earshot, everyone had another go at the version we'd all grown up with.

I'll sing you twelve songs; Green grow the rushes—o.
What are your twelve songs?
Twelve for the goblins woken;

Eleven for the pigs that learned to fly, and
Ten for the pixies' tokens;
Nine for the promise spoken;
Eight for the hearts bespoken;
Seven for the lovers that said goodbye, and
Six for the spirits broken;
Five, for the wish-stars in the sky, and
Four for the loves unspoken.
Three, three, hearts blee-ee-ee-eed SO!
Two, true as lily-white swans; drifting where the waters flow.
One is one and all alone and evermore shall be so.

Except that this time around, some lines had changed to yet another version by the time we reached the end and Kes was out of hearing. After that the songs grew coarser.

Storm knew a lot of those.

Day Seven

Robin

The morning after Eden Thatcher roused me from my apathy, Cris came with Kip before school to tell me about Brook's interrogation. Eden had arrived while Kip was at school the previous afternoon.

"Eden already knows a lot about us according to Brook – about the bad feeling between Jay and Ira, and us owing money, and the rumours, and you not following Ira's craft."

"Is that meant to be something we argued about? Ira's never cared if I prepared potions or taught tarlings for a living. I could offer better reasons than that for disposing of the old tyrant!"

Cris's jaw fell. "I hope you didn't, pet."

"Oh, for heaven's sake!" Kip frowned at Cris. "Brook said Eden was just being thorough. No investigator worth a spark would let themselves be railroaded into quick conclusions by the likes of Jess."

"Or us," Cris added.

"Or us," agreed Kip. "Now I'd better go and open up. I'll drop in after school, and you can let me know later if there are any developments."

When Kip had gone, our eyes met. Neither of us was reassured by Brook's reading of Eden. Brook had always been an over-generous judge of character.

"What did *you* think, Rob?"

"You didn't meet Eden then?"

"No. I was out ordering charcoal."

I shook my head. "I'm frightened, Cris. We know Jay is harmless. Everyone in Fendle knows it, including Jess and Taz, if they weren't such rumour-mongers."

"Well, mostly Jess."

"Jay doesn't even get angry." Not properly angry. There had been times when I had wished…

"Except with Ira," Cris reminded me, and I recalled a shouting match last summer across the parlour of the Barley Mow when my wages went missing. No doubt Eden will have heard about it.

"Jay doesn't even know this is happening."

"No," Cris agreed. "You're right, pet; Jay ought to be told. There could be a simple explanation for the knife being here. Might Ira have borrowed it?"

That seemed as unlikely as every other "might" I had dreamed up, but at least Cris was thinking along the same lines as me. And had made a decision.

"I'll go to Wendle and warn Jay what to expect. The fair opens today. I can get there before it's over."

What then? Surely, Jay would return to face the accusations. My life remained on hold until Ira turned up. Or until Jay came back.

Or not.

At some point in that endless day, a new fancy presented itself. If I had known Kip would be so keen to take my class, I might have gone to the fair with Jay.

When would anyone have known Ira was missing?

I recalled the afternoon of the open door and the empty cottage. With no-one to feed Fern, she might have wandered off in search of food. Her pups would follow her… Probably only to the forge, though. She couldn't hunt with her deformed leg.

I loved Fern with her deformity. How could I be so sure that nobody would love me with mine? So certain that I must cling to Jay.

Whose knife was found in our deserted cottage.

I imagined Kip on the way home from school, noticing the cottage door open, or stopping anyway to check in, and finding Ira gone. And the knife.

If Cris came to us at the fair to warn about the knife, would we return to face the accusations? (Staying away would suggest the lies were true though.)

Or would we let them think what they liked? We'd be well out of it.

The memory of our last meeting brought me back to earth. That, and the difficulties I now had connecting. I couldn't ignore the possibility that Jay was deliberately shutting me out.

Rather than spend my days in a half-dream, it was time I returned to work.

Jay

The first morning of the fair dawned with a clear blue sky. A light mist was rising as we set out our wares. I'd been up with the songbirds, changed my tunic three times and my earrings twice. I buzzed like a beehive.

Young Kestrel was scrupulously comparing necklets when Storm appeared, strolling across the field untidy as ever, but looking good, being one of those annoying people who'd look good in a sack. Progress was leisurely, greeting people on the way and enjoying the morning sun as it broke through. I hadn't thought to see Storm this early.

I'd been looking out anyway.

"And how are you this bright, sunny morning? What have you to sell me?"

Storm had nothing to pay with and was living on the goodwill of the Seagen, but I answered in kind.

"Pattern and plate, cogs and keys, tools and trinkets, keen arrowheads to kill a rabbit and sharp knives to skin it."

"Fine bangles and neck charms," added Kestrel, showing off the pair finally selected.

"D'you know, I do believe those are nicer than mine. Would you be wanting to swap them?"

They admired each other's armlets until Mikki appeared with a needless remark about children's pleasures and called me to talk to a Wenn farmer interested in scythes. I left to discuss discounts and delivery times.

To my delight, Storm was still there when I got back.

I put the apprentices in charge of the stall, made sure Danni understood about recording sales, told Mikki where to find me if needed, and we set off to tour the Wenn Fair.

The sun was still with us, but as the breeze freshened, clouds were gathering. The stalls held little I hadn't seen before, but everything fascinated Storm. I checked out our rivals from other villages. The Tarfen smiths had fetters and chained wrist cuffs among the usual tools and trappings, which might interest our cousins, the Wysmiths, at Fendle's main forge. According to the stall keeper, a new Minstrers' department helped design them for restraining prisoners on their way to Advisors' judgement, or to the stocks or the gallows. On reflection, I didn't see much call for them in Fendle.

Then Kyl came for me. Mikki had another customer who wanted my attention.

Storm didn't come with me. "I'll see you later. I'm thinking I'll do some exploring."

I admitted I'd be busy for most of the day and grudgingly went with Kyl.

After speaking to the customer, I reckoned Mikki would have managed well enough without me, but I hid my annoyance and joined Danni cleaning the silver. Storm came by soon after, leading a small bay mount with white blaze and socks. I'm no judge of horseflesh, but even I could tell it wasn't a carthorse.

"I'm off to explore High Wenn. Will I be seeing you later at the Green Man? They're rigging a shelter to the front of it."

"Oh good! They won't want to lose trade when it rains again." We'd already lost the sun behind gathering grey. "You might get caught it. Whose is the horse?"

"This is Blaze. Little beauty, isn't he?"

Little he wasn't, but he was indeed beautiful. Storm patted his neck affectionately. "Opal's family lent him when we stopped there on the way."

I was impressed. The Llann weren't noted for their generosity. But they'd know by now their horse was in good hands. Seagen and Llann travelled together from the mountain pass, and I'd heard scraps last night of how the foreigner's knack with horses had proved useful more than once.

Storm's nose wrinkled. "What's that stuff you're using on the silver? It smells disgusting!"

Danni smirked and raised it closer.

"Silver-tonic. Robin makes it. It's good for cleaning any metal but it's magic on silver. You get used to the smell."

"I'll take your word for it." Storm turned back to me. "Would that be Robin with the cantankerous parent you were telling me about?"

"That's the one – taught Rob how to mix all kinds of potions and gunges. Some are for healing, and some are good for cleaning things. And some just smell nice."

"Not that one," Storm said. "I'll be seeing you later, then."

I watched them leave the fair's ground and started following the sun's progress toward later. I had hopes of later.

Day Eight

Robin

Kip stopped by on the way to school to report that Cris left for Wendale that morning. I said I ought to go back to work.

I must have sounded as uncertain as I felt because Kip suggested I take another day. We agreed to go in together tomorrow and see how things went from there.

Around lunchtime, Eden Thatcher arrived on my doorstep. I managed a civil greeting, but inside I quailed.

I scanned the floor for puppy mess before inviting the Administrator in. I offered a drink, omitting the gooseberry wine, which I had finished the night before. This time, tea was accepted.

The leather bag was in evidence, but nothing had yet been produced from it. I busied myself boiling water while Eden spoke.

"I understand that the searchers mostly searched the roads to the village, so I've organised a wider search."

"Well, Ira never walked far… and it rained non-stop last week."

Eden blinked twice as the pale lips stretched briefly. I nearly dropped the kettle, but decided it was a patronising smile.

"I know it's unlikely that Ira walked far, but we have to search. We've been over the ground already covered," the implication being that it wouldn't have been searched properly, "in case we find something to help us understand what happened."

"Ira's walking stick," I thought aloud.

"Yes. It would be helpful to find that."

I offered apple, rosehip and mint or chamomile tea. Eden chose apple and rosehip. I wondered where else they might usefully search as I poured water in the pot and covered it with the cosy. I took cups and teapot to the table and sat.

Eden began informally but lapsed into something more like an official statement.

"I know you're concerned for your friend, so I'm here to put your mind at rest. I have spoken to people who witnessed Jay Cutler's wagon return to the village that afternoon and proceed directly to Cutler's Forge. On leaving again, it was seen to follow the same route out of Fendle. Since School Lane is a dead end, the wagon couldn't come into it by another route, but we have further sightings of Jay anyway, far enough out to preclude a return on foot within the timeframe."

I took a deep breath – my first for some time – and reprocessed what I'd just heard, to make sure I'd got it right. Eden watched as if unsure I had followed the argument. I returned the gaze, still looking for a catch.

"So, Jay is no longer a suspect."

The eyes smiled. They were quite nice hazel eyes, after all. The thin lips remained expressionless, but I could have kissed them. The thought of Eden's shock if I had, made me hiccough. It started as a laugh, but I swallowed it. Hilarity might be an unwise reaction. As far as I knew, I had yet to be ruled out as a suspect myself.

The relief was overwhelming.

I closed the door behind Eden and leaned against it, feeling weightless. Time for a celebration; I regretted finishing that gooseberry wine prematurely.

I stepped away from the door, and my feet took over, setting to my partner (Fern) in steps I'd often watched in the dance but never attempted in public. Fern bowed her front end with her rump in the air, tail wagging. She barked, and the pups came yapping to join the dance. I made my way through them to collapse gratefully into Ira's fireside chair.

Thankless, unfeeling child that I was, I gave no thought to my missing parent. I had to find Jay.

With hope but little expectation, I sent out my happy thoughts to share.

Perhaps my exhilaration was the impetus needed to cover the distance and break through barriers. This time, I got through.

Jay

I organised a duty rota to wangle myself that morning off and the next. The rain had stopped, and wispy clouds mottled the pale sky.

We spread a blanket outside the fair's main entrance and watched as the path grew busier. Wenlings were earning pocket-money by minding the horses tethered in a neighbouring field. Carts and carriages waited along the roadside. A queue formed for a fortune teller who'd set up a screen near the gate with two stools behind it.

Other locals had set up pitches selling food. I suspected the innkeeper might be unhappy about those, especially the stall selling barley wine. We were sipping ours when Storm asked, "Is there a horse you could ride to go exploring?"

"They're all draught horses. Swift's lighter – the one pulling the new cart – and he's used to being ridden. I can take him."

"Do that then and we'll ride out tomorrow, since you've the day free."

I smiled back and for a moment, our eyes held until something flipped in my throat and my nerve faltered. Hoping my voice sounded normal, I studied my drink.

"I'd like that. The fair brings me here twice a year, but I've never been past High Wenn."

"We'll try shadeward then. Neither of us came in that way. New territory."

New territory sounded promising. Had Storm's voice softened or slowed? Or was that only in my mind? I was unsure as a school 'ling pining for a classmate. Away from the fair, there'd be no-one to see if I made a fool of myself.

The sun had climbed as high as it was likely to; it was nearly time for my afternoon shift. We finished our barley wine, and Storm nodded towards the fortune teller's pitch. The queue had gone.

"We could go have our fortunes read some time."

"Let's do it now."

Storm eyed me thoughtfully. "You're not one for putting things off, are you now?"

"Might not be here tomorrow," I said.

Eyebrows lifted.

"The fortune teller," I said. What else would I have meant?

I was first behind the fortune teller's screen. Storm waited at the point marked for queueing, just out of earshot. The heavily veiled figure was stooped and faintly laughable, but I didn't want to upset the old Wenn. I crossed the palm held out for my coin, settled on the stool, and offered my hand. The hunched figure grasped it firmly while looking into my eyes. Apparently satisfied, the seer turned its attention to my palm. The shrouded skull sunk lower into the heap of wraps and the entire mass hunkered into itself, like a moulting owl, but the hand supporting mine was warm and dry.

Low, rhythmical tones delivered some flattering prose about my kind nature and my future wealth, and I waited to hear that I would meet a tall, dark stranger (I was ahead of the fortune teller on that one). Instead, the mystic looked into my eyes again, as if checking it was still me, and delivered a final judgement.

"You have much to learn. You are not ready for the one that destiny has chosen for you."

Disappointing, but that was all I'd be getting. The soothsayer drew itself up to its full height to show me out. (Unexpectedly, our eyes were level. I'd thought the seer shorter.)

Now it was Storm's turn.

The fortune teller stood eye-to-eye with Storm too, after their session ended – a good trick, made easier by all that shrouding. I'd provided a coin for the scrying, since Storm had none, but afterwards it was returned to me. The fortune teller forgot to ask for it.

Storm seemed subdued and didn't ask what I'd been told, so I didn't feel I could ask either. As we passed through the gate into the field, I sensed a mental shake, like a dog shakes off water, and Storm was back.

Only the blue eyes were heavier. "I'm off for a ride. I'll be seeing you later?"

"Of course. I'm not going anywhere."

I read an understanding in the answering smile which lifted me for the rest of the afternoon.

On the stall, thoughts of spending the next day together lifted me from the mundane business of trading, and I may have let one or two items go for less than I would normally haggle for. I was deep into one wildly hopeful daydream when I sensed that Robin was there too.

Oops!

That brought me back to the marketplace with a bump. Robin had withdrawn, and I busied myself selling a knife to a customer who'd come to buy earrings. I expect Robin saved us a few sales that afternoon.

Day Nine

Robin

I had eavesdropped on stronger feelings than I had believed Jay capable of… passion, yearning for someone – who wasn't me – and, worst of all, anticipation. The shock was almost physical. My mind backed away, and I folded onto a chair, physically curling around the pain.

It led to another sleepless night between telling myself this was just another infatuation and telling myself it didn't matter. Hadn't I decided to move on?

I was accustomed to coping with three in our relationship. Until now, the third had never lasted long. This felt different. By morning I had acknowledged the unavoidable truth. Jay didn't feel that way about me. Never had. Never would.

Although I had pictured a future without Jay, I hadn't believed in it. Now Jay's absence in that picture hurt like a severed limb that continues to ache.

I dragged myself back to my immediate future. Today that would be the schoolroom. Waiting in the cottage for Kip to arrive, I ate breakfast, washed up the breakfast things, wiped them dry, wiped down the table, wiped down the worktops… The food sat like a stone in my stomach.

Kip stayed with me all day, and we took the class together. The tarlings were more manageable with two of us. Fin was quiet – not the usual silent subversion but seeming distracted. That minor change made a difference to the entire class. Away from Fin's shadow, Cay had blossomed and was revelling in the role of adviser to the younger tarlings. A fresh scar on one arm was worrying though. Cay dismissed it as a thorn scratch and kept tugging the sleeve over it.

At the end of the day, Kip told the class it had been a pleasure teaching them and seemed to mean it.

When we got to the cottage, Eden and Brook were waiting for us. Ira had been found.

Jay

Last night was another heady, disappointing evening. We'd joined wholeheartedly in the drinking, and the arms-across-shoulders singing, and continued to lean against each other when the songs ended. We were still singing as we weaved our way back from the tavern. On reaching the point where our paths parted, Storm had pecked my cheek and slurred, "Night, darlin. See you in the mornin," and wandered off towards the Seagen quarter.

So, I told myself not to expect too much from our morning ride, but I don't think I was listening.

I returned from collecting Swift to find Mikki and the youngsters watching Storm struggle to open a wooden puzzle – something the locksmiths' apprentice had devised.

Puzzles sold well to those wealthy enough to have time to play with them. This one featured hidden cogs which had to be positioned a certain way to release a catch. In theory, a metal version could be used to lock chains or rings together, but once the sequence was discovered, it would be easy to open. Mikki's grin grew wider at each failed attempt.

Storm twisted it this way and that. "Are there instructions for it?"

"There are. Each one's different, so we have to make sure we give out the right ones."

"I know someone who'd love one of these. Are the directions easy to follow?"

"Dead easy," said Danni. "Foolproof."

"First find your fool," murmured Mikki, turning aside to a customer.

I judged it time we went.

We couldn't wander far; I had to be back in time for the afternoon's bidding. We chatted about nothing much and enjoyed the gentle sun. To one side of us, tiny brown birds hovered over the fields, rising and falling and twittering frantically as if sound alone would keep them airborne. Others burbled from the reeds along the river.

Storm wanted to keep to the river path. "It doesn't take long to get lost in a forest." Further along, though, where the river ran into woodland, the track led away from the river. A magpie flew down from the trees and landed on the path ahead.

"One for sorrow." Said Storm sadly, as if the rhyme were a prediction.

"You're as bad as Brook," I teased. "Look, there are more." Two others had joined the first. "That's three for a soulmate."

"Is it?" Storm's eyebrows rose. "That's another rhyme we learned different, then. How does yours go?"

I recited:

One for sorrow, two for joy,
Three for a soulmate, four for a toy.
Five for silver, six for gold,
Seven for a secret never to be told.

"How does yours go?"

Storm chanted:

One for sorrow, two for mirth,
Three for a bedding, four for a birth.
Five for silver, six for gold,
Seven for a new corpse, stiff and cold.

"That's a bit grim. I think I prefer ours. Oh, look, there's another one."

"One of the others has taken off, though. Does it still count?"

All meaningless drivel, but I didn't dare begin the conversation I wanted to have.

We began singing songs from the previous night. After initial confusion, we discovered we were both inclined to harmonise, so agreed to take turns singing melody or harmony. At the end of one spirited rendering, I detected a background roar behind the twittering of birds and the yipping of tree-rats. As we moved on, it grew louder.

Storm recognised it. "A waterfall! Come on."

Where the path ahead diverged, we took the track heading towards the sound. A glimpse of water glistened, and we were out of the trees again. Below us, water tumbled over rocks from further up the hill into a small lake. To call it a waterfall may have been an exaggeration.

It was probably nothing spectacular by Llannoc standards, but we don't get waterfalls in Tarn.

Storm dismounted and slithered down the bank to the lake.

"Let's swim."

I followed. "It looks bloody freezing."

Already Storm was pulling off clothing, and I didn't want to spoil the moment, but the day wasn't that warm, even allowing for the sun being on our side of the lake.

I peeled off my top layer in a spirit of investigation.

"You can swim?" Storm thought to ask.

"Just about. I'm not a strong swimmer."

Storm smiled into my eyes. "I'll keep you safe."

I wanted to believe.

Storm entered the water like an arrow, slender and pale. I whimpered.

My less elegant jump drew a gasp. It was bloody freezing.

When I was able to register my surroundings again, Storm was halfway to the other side of the lake.

I splashed around the nearer bank while Storm swam effortlessly back to shallower water and stood to walk the last few paces. I ached for this lean and graceful body that curved and arched in all the right places. I wanted it so badly…

…and maybe it wasn't just me. Storm's eyes were dark as they roamed my body.

"You've goose pimples! Come on, out with you and dry off."

When I turned to face my tormentor, who was busy rubbing me down with an over-tunic, our arms somehow slid around each other. Our eyes locked and my heart thumped hard enough to be felt where we pressed together.

After a preliminary croak, Storm said, "We have to get you dressed."

"Do we?" It wasn't what I had in mind at all. "I'm feeling warmer already."

"Oh, Jay…" Storm's forehead creased. Indigo-dark eyes looked to the sky… where the sun had reached its peak between the tops of the nearest trees.

"Sheil! The bidding! I could–"

"No, you couldn't. I'll get the blame if you're not there. I'm not Mikki's favourite fairgoer as it is."

"Stuff Mikki!" I exploded. With feeling.

But my family would have my toenails for tiddlywinks if I didn't come back with a decent return for their borrowed money.

I started haphazardly pulling on the nearest garment until Storm gently took it from me and gave me my own.

When we were both covered and inaccessible, Storm pulled me close. We kissed long and deep. It wasn't steamy with passion. It was a promise. Even so, had it happened a shadow's shift earlier I'd have forgotten about the fair and the stalls and to hell with the bidding.

The bidding!

Bidding took place over two afternoons, and that would be the most pressing of my obligations. Danni and Kyl knew their way about the stall now. Mikki might protest but knew as much as I did about delivery times and more than I did about carriage springs.

"They won't need me after tomorrow. Let's take a couple of days away. We can camp by the lake."

"As long as the skies don't open again."

I ignored that and carried on planning.

"I'll need to be at the bidding tomorrow. If I take another day to work my share and tie things up with Mikki,

I can leave them to deal with the stalls for a couple of days. We could be away for two nights and then back on the last day. I can tidy any loose ends while we're packing up the day after."

Storm's smile was like the sun rising.

A decision had been made, and not only about our camping trip. After tomorrow we'd have two whole days and nights to ourselves.

But I was confident I wouldn't have to wait that long

PART TWO: Partings

Day Ten, Jay

WOW!

Birds were celebrating overhead. I opened my eyes on sunlight dappling the ground. The air in the copse blew morning fresh, but we were cosy under my cover with Storm curved snug against my back. As I touched the arm lying across me, it tightened, and Storm's nose nuzzled my neck. I turned, and we regarded each other before kissing gently.

Now I was awake, my thoughts tumbled over each other. I shared them with Storm.

"If I'm going to disappear for two days, I'll have to give the youngsters some time off first." Storm kissed my nose.

"So I won't be able to get away from the stall at all." Storm kissed one side of my mouth. "Not for the next couple of days."

Storm kissed the other side and said, "But tonight?"

"I thought you'd never ask."

Storm kissed my mouth, and I returned the kiss before saying, "No, really. I began to think you–"

Storm said, "Shh," and kissed my mouth again. Then nobody said anything for a while.

"I was trying to be… sensible," Storm said. "We both have homes to go to."

"Don't remind me. I come here to get away from mine. Don't worry about me, love. I can look after myself. I'm a grown Tarn."

One of Storm's eyebrows rose.

"I can vouch for that, darlin."

Then we made memories until it was time to face the day.

Samphire was setting out their stall as we passed the Seagen quarter. Kestrel wore a sullen scowl. We caught the end of Sam's words. "I've nothing more to say on the subject."

Kes spotted us and appealed for support. "I want to see a boar hunt, but I'm not allowed."

"Samphire's right," I said. "It's dangerous. You know Mikki? Well, Mikki's partner got killed in one of those boar hunts."

"Boar are powerful, so they are, and vicious beasts when they're angry."

Behind this apparent warning, I detected unholy relish, and a chill flushed down my spine. I'd found Storm yesterday at the boar hunt stand in the Wendale quarter, next to the stall that sold spears.

"They wouldn't take you out anyway, Kes," I said. "Not even with a grown-up looking after you." I couldn't recall how old you had to be, but I was confident it would be older than Kes.

The spratling admitted sadly, "That's what the fortune-teller told me too."

"You've been to the fortune-teller?" Storm's eyes widened extravagantly. "The one who sits outside the fair's ground?" Kestrel nodded and Sam added, "Aye, the dwarf with a pitch outside main gate. Is there another?"

I shook my head. "The one outside the gate's the only pitch I've seen, although there might be a couple of them taking turns. I'd better get to my pitch. See you later."

Mikki's head shook on seeing me walking back from the Seagen quarter carrying my blanket. I shook my head back at Mikki, who stood beside a Tarn from Tarfen called Laurel outside the new wagon which they'd commandeered as sleeping quarters. Danni and friend had been sleeping under it, and Kyl was away somewhere with a young Wenn while I had the second wagon to myself. I hadn't brought Storm there last night.

Laurel took leave of Mikki and as our paths crossed, I took the opportunity to ask, "Have you any idea what Mikki's got against Storm?"

I was answered with a sympathetic smile. I liked this one. Laurel can't have been much younger than Mikki but, like Mikki, was wearing well.

"Don't take it to heart. I think Mikki was getting worried about your priorities, but now the pair of you've got together, you might find mother hen easing off on the clucking."

That would be a relief.

They'd been talking about us then.

"I hope you're right. I'm about to suggest that Mikki takes a couple of days off, so that I can take the two days after. Things are quietening down now, and the youngsters can run the stalls while I'm at the bidding. Mikki might be at a loose end."

"Thanks for telling me. I'll see if I can negotiate some time off."

We headed off to our separate negotiations, and I thought that Storm and I might stay in the wagon tonight.

If we stayed quiet.

Although that hollow between the bushes hadn't been uncomfortable.

Day Ten, Robin

Kip went back into school for me, and I spent the morning at Cutler's Forge. Ira's body lay in the room that used to be our room. It would lay there now until its burning.

They had found Ira lying face-up among reeds at the river's edge, but with head and shoulders under water. After eight days, I could do little to conceal the damage, but I dressed the body in clothes I brought with me, veiling what was left of Ira's face.

When I secured that dilapidated hat, the body became Ira, and not just a featureless corpse.

Brook joined me as I arranged sweet-smelling herbs to freshen the room.

"It was eerie, Robin, like a river-demon lying there." Brook shuddered. "I stayed while Elm went to find the others. We weren't to touch anything until Eden had seen."

River creatures had visited Ira's body, but no wound looked to have been made by a knife. Whoever's blood was on Jay's knife, it wasn't Ira's.

"There's no knife wound anywhere," I said.

"I know. Eden looked for cuts when we pulled the body out of the water. A rope was caught around the feet, holding them out of the water. Otherwise, Ira might have been able to stand up. It was tying a rotten eel trap to a bush. Eden thought the trap could have been on the bank and Ira's fall knocked it in the water, tightening the coil. A branch was snapped off the bush. Ira might have grabbed at it while falling."

"Hello Brook, Robin." Eden stood in the doorway. "Don't let me interrupt. I'm not staying. I've been to the Barley Mow and my next stop is the forge to thank everyone who helped search."

Brook's head shook slowly. "I hadn't expected to find Ira there, though, drowned like Sal and Aspen."

I struggled to understand why. "Why go there in the first place? And why so close to the river? Why not take the path?"

"There is no path," said Eden. "If there ever was one it's overgrown."

"I suppose nobody goes that way now." Fin and Cay lived in that direction, but they always cut through Cutler's Forge.

"The rope had been there a while too," said Eden. "Grass had grown over it."

"When Sal was alive, Ira would take me along the river there to find wildflowers for potions."

"Ira's family were apothecaries," Brook explained, although I'm sure Eden would have been aware of that by now. "We go to Ira and Robin for our remedies."

"I hope you still will. Ira must have taught me all the brews over the years."

I explained to Eden. "We don't make them to sell. Just for ourselves and friends. There's a new apothecary in Fendle now, and I don't want to take their trade."

Eden seemed impressed, nonetheless.

"We've never enough healers in Tarfen." It seemed a sore point. "Generations after the Sickness, you still can't find one when you want one."

"Oh, I'm not a healer. I just know how to prepare the mixtures and what they're used for. Have you been ill then?"

"Not me. Ro was ill in the summer; one of those childhood fevers they catch from each other. It's always a worry."

Ro?

Brook enlightened me. "Eden has a nine-year tarling."

Why did that surprise me? Eden was old enough to have several – had probably been settled for half a lifetime.

This detour into personal territory prompted a return to formality. Eden straightened.

"I ought to get on. I gather Taz has plans for me this afternoon."

"Lucky you."

Brook's sympathy provoked a rare smile from Eden. The two were easy together. Each had taken the other's measure at some earlier meeting and approved what they found. After Eden left, Brook turned to practical matters.

"Don't worry about the arrangements for Ira's burning. We'll set the pyre and tell people when it's happening."

"You and Kip have done so much already. Kip's been shiel-sent. I couldn't have coped with work this last week. How are you managing at the forge?"

"Mustn't grumble. It's worth it to see Kip so sunny every morning, looking forward to the day ahead. It must have been difficult for you, though, not knowing."

"Yes. At least now we know, even if we don't know why. I'm still in shock, I think. The cottage is unnaturally peaceful."

"You have been in a kind of daze since Ira disappeared, as if you were looking for a direction to take."

"Ah. You noticed that."

"Well... we know you."

We didn't talk about the mystery of the knife, still unsolved, but no longer looming so darkly. Brook looked younger today. I felt different, too. Breathing was easier, and my body seemed lighter.

Brook's release was more justified than mine. The discovery of my parent's body should surely have filled me with grief, not relief.

I was free now to decide what direction I should take.

Eden was leaving the workshop as I walked through the yard.

"Shall I walk you home?"

"You don't have to." I hadn't meant to sound so churlish. "You can if you want." Not much better. "Thank you for finding Ira. I'm sorry if I seemed... irritable."

"You've been worried."

We fell into step. Eden's long legs must have been holding back to match my speed, but it didn't feel that way, as it sometimes did walking with Jay.

The conversational pace was less comfortable. I wished I had waited longer before leaving Brook, or that Eden had been less scrupulous about offering to walk me home. The day was pleasant, and I would have enjoyed the walk without having to make conversation.

A cloud of starlings swooped noisily overhead. They touched down in one of the fields before taking off again in a single fluttering shadow. Watching them, I missed my footing and Eden took my arm in a firm grip, quickly released when I steadied.

So I felt enough of an idiot already without fumbling the heavy key to my front door. The lock never caused me problems before. As the door opened, Eden's bemused voice came from behind me.

"There's a dog here." I turned to see the stray that hangs around the forge, sitting patiently behind us. "It just came from behind the house. I'm sure I saw it at the forge earlier. Is it anything to do with you?"

"I think it might be," I admitted. "Let him come in then."

Fern greeted her visitor, who was immediately surrounded by his puppies. I doubt he knew they were his puppies. They were nearly as tall as him already, but their legs were unlikely to grow as long as Fern's.

"Surely not," said Eden, looking from Fern to the crossbreed terrier.

"You'd be surprised," I said.

I looked up and I swear Eden was blushing.

The dog knew exactly where to find Fern's rear exit, but soon came indoors again. Unlike Fern, he was spry enough to jump the fence.

"That must be how he got in before." I told Eden.

He'd had the sense not to come in while Ira was at home. Perhaps he'd got in originally when we were at the forge or out collecting ingredients.

I stood at the open door as Eden left. The sky wasn't heavy, but the mild autumn air smelled fresh, as if charged with rain. Gripped by a restless energy that must be spent, I scrubbed the cottage as it hadn't been scrubbed since we moved in. Table and floors were swept and scoured; spiders were made homeless. I changed Fern's bedding and mine, swept the hearth, and chopped wood to replenish the stack.

When I finished, the sink gleamed, and the pots sparkled. Then I added rosemary to the room's fragrance – small changes can make a big difference – mended a broken window catch, put up two more hooks for kitchen tools and hung Kip's drawing of Fern that I'd framed before Ira disappeared.

Halfway through this orgy of activity, I closed the door as the shower started. Later, after I fed us all, the rain stopped, and the little dog stood to be let out. His tail waved goodbye as he scampered between puddles towards the forge, probably in search of another supper.

Then I went early to bed and slept more soundly than I had since childhood.

Day Twelve

Jay

For two days we had only our evenings together. But I would know if Storm was on the fair's ground or out riding the countryside, just as I knew without turning when the blue eyes were watching me. If our hands couldn't touch, our spirits could.

On the morning we left the fair we were up at early light. Danni was stirring and Hawk padded from Mikki's cart to see us off. No sound came from inside the wagon. We passed Kyl trailing through the morning mist and yawning widely.

Storm quickly saddled Blaze and checked Swift's straps as I finished fastening them. I was slower and Storm was restless.

Wennfolk were setting up pitches outside, their early morning voices low as we left the fair behind with two whole days ahead of us.

Away from the fair, only the soft thump of our mounts' hooves and the birds' singing broke the silence. Our voices would have seemed a violation. The lake was half a morning's journey, but we had no reason to hurry. This world was ours alone for today and tomorrow. The day after that was a distant cloud on the horizon.

Wenn forests are vaster than Tarn's woodlands, gnarled and ancient. Today the sky was blue again as sun broke through the haze with a promise of warmth later. We rode through leaves that fell from the trees whenever a tree-rat shook the bough, or a heavy bird landed. Soon the only leaves left on the trees would be evergreens and reds – the colours of winter.

At the lake, we found a spot along the river's edge where the horses could reach water and left them to graze while we made camp. Storm went to dig a trap in a likely spot while I built a fire to light later.

Housekeeping done, we sat with our backs against a tree wide enough to support us both. We'd brought bread, cheese, and barley wine. Storm draped an arm comfortably across my shoulders and lifted the flask to drink before handing it to me. I re-corked the flask and placed it carefully on the ground so that we could kiss slowly, lingering in the manner of people who have all day before them, and some more. Storm tasted of barley wine.

When we parted, Storm uncorked the flask again. Dragonflies came to investigate, returning to dart and hover at the lake.

"We might catch a couple of fish for later. I saw some fat carp in there when we were swimming."

Fishing hadn't been one of my accomplishments. "We didn't bring any nets."

"Heron by name, heron by nature." Storm scanned the forest floor. "A sharpened stick'll do. A strong straight branch and a good knife to sharpen it."

Storm's knife came from Scarth, heavy but sharp enough. I'd brought one of Elm's with me. Before joining us at the forge, Elm had been a smith by birth – a second or third cousin – and this was a light, strong blade, not unlike my own. If I should ever find it again.

A stab of unease reminded me that this hunting knife was another sale I wouldn't be making. Storm wore my bangle and pendant every day. I didn't grudge them, nor the silver earrings, but could I have done more to boost our profits? My mind had been elsewhere.

The bidding had gone well, and I'd secured all we needed at a good price. The money had taken less time to spend than it would take to pay back...

I shook off the untimely nudgings of conscience and offered Storm my services, such as they were.

"I can supply a sharp knife, but as far as catching anything... More sparrow than heron, I'm afraid. That's about my mark – insects and caterpillars."

"That'll do, or a worm. I can catch us a fish by hand. If you find us the bait, I'll look for a likely spot to draggle it."

"I've not seen that done. Our fishers use traps and nets. The 'lings catch things with lines and bent pins, but they have the time to wait."

"It just takes patience and a quick hand, and some practice to judge when to grab. As scarlings, we'd spend whole days at the river. Every year I'd be in trouble for fishing when I shouldn't."

"*??*"

"When the fish are breeding," Storm explained, seeing my puzzled expression. It didn't help. "You're not supposed to catch fish when they're breeding. They'd forget to remind the scarlings when the time came, and the Guardians would catch us and fine our families."

"We haven't any rules like tRobinRobinhat. Is it another one of your Wardens' laws, then?"

During evenings in front of the Green Man, Storm had told us about the Wardens of Scarth and the Guardians who upheld their laws. The Wardens governed much as the Advisors presided over Tarn. They'd once claimed to interpret the laws of the gods, but I'd got the impression that Scarthers didn't take their gods any more seriously than we took the shiel. Storm confirmed as much.

"Most of the old laws make sense if you know why they're there, but I reckon some of 'em are just a ways to get extra fines off us. Nobody tries telling us now that the laws come from the gods.

The Wardens' authority is supposed to come from old records kept in the Temple that go back forever, inscribed in tiny, black, letters on sheets of thin, white parchment, smoother than skin, that lie flat together, fixed between boards. They're not just rules, though. They tell of old disasters, plagues and worse, long ages before the last Sickness."

"You had the Sickness too?"

"I think it's in the land beneath us. Or maybe in the air… It killed off whole villages, so they say." Storm had fallen into storyteller style. "In times of Sickness, the Wardens shut themselves in the Temple and banish anyone who shows signs of the Sickness. They claim their survival is for the greater good. Last time, they took the best of the healers into shelter with them and enough Guardians to protect the Temple."

"So, your Guardians are like Temple guards?"

"They were then. They're based in the towns now, although they patrol the villages too. They collect Temple taxes and authorise the healers and generally maintain order."

"Your healers have to be authorised? I know a bit about herbs and potions I've picked up from Robin. What if I tried to help someone?"

"It'd be sensible to keep quiet about that if you didn't want to be accused of witchcraft. You often speak of Robin. Tell me about Robin."

"Do I? Well, we grew up together. We're close."

I was about to say, like siblings, but was that a hint of jealousy in Storm's voice?

I did hope so.

Robin

It was my place, as Ira's closest kin, to invoke the sheil of passage. The flames would free Ira's spirit for the shiel to guide it to rest and reconciliation, in preparation for rebirth.

As the sky lightened, I recited the brief incantation and touched my torch to the places Elm had marked for me. The fire quickly caught and spread. I smiled my relief and gratitude to Brook and Elm. There would be little left to collect for burial when the pyre cooled.

It was a family occasion, even though Ira wasn't a Cutler. I wished the whole family could be with us, especially now that Cris's mission was no longer necessary. Kip had sent a message to Wendale fairground by pigeon, for the attention of Cris, Jay or Mikki, to say that Ira's body had been found and Jay was no longer under suspicion. We could only hope the pigeon would arrive safely and in time.

Had it not been for the rumours that followed Ira's disappearance, I doubt we would have seen so many villagers at the burning. Since there were, I would make sure they all knew that Ira's death owed nothing to anyone's knife.

Villagers came to declare sympathy for my loss, but few found anything positive to say about the departed. After half a life spent in bitterness and anger, Ira's shade would have much to reconcile. Few seemed to remember the good work the Hawns did before Sal's death, and the people they had helped. Reputations were easily damaged in Fendle and hard to redeem.

Annis Reaper was one of the few whose words of commiseration rang true, and I remembered Annis's partner had recently died. The couple had known my parents well. Their eldest tarling was born the same year as Aspen. I heard the siblings had recently taken over running of the farm, but though Annis's long hair was white now, the kindly eyes were still clear and sharp. People still listened to what Annis had to say.

Kip left to take my class, and I expected most of the villagers to leave as well, but instead more arrived. They wouldn't be missing work out of respect for Ira. More likely, they were here to make sure the old devil was really gone and not about to rise from the pyre, stick waving, to curse them all.

They stood in groups, murmuring together. I glanced around the field and caught the echo of more than one suspicious gaze, averted late. Brook came to stand by me.

"How are you, Robin?"

"Uncomfortable. I feel like a fraud. People are offering sympathy and I have no grief. I am unnatural."

"It'll catch you later. I thought I was coping when my parents died, but it was half a year later when it hit me." Brook's eyes glistened. "I disintegrated over an old scoreboard of a game we used to play."

"You still feel it, don't you?"

A smile warmed the unshed tears. "Mustn't grumble. At least they went within days of each other."

"You were close to yours, weren't you," I said. *Not like Ira and me.*

"At the time, it was almost a relief. When someone's in constant pain, you can't hope for them to go on living with it."

"I suppose not." I tried to be charitable. "There are different kinds of pain. Ira lost the will to live when Sal and Aspen died."

Or, at least, the will to stay conscious. A hand rested a moment on my shoulder, and then Brook returned to practicalities.

"Don't worry about tomorrow. We'll collect the ashes. If you're happy for us to take care of it, we'll prepare Ira's grave as well."

Fendle's burial field is by the river. Dig down around any village and you're likely to hit a layer of rubble, so a field is better. Grass soon grows over, and animals can graze to stop it from getting overgrown.

"I'll appreciate your help, Brook, but I want to dig with you. I won't be a lot of use, but it might help convince me that Ira's gone."

"Come for dinner tomorrow after school, and we'll fix a time."

"The sooner, the better?" I ventured, and Brook smiled back at me.

Eden came to express condolences, which I accepted as formally as they were offered. Brook's greeting was warm and was returned in kind. The three of us fed the pyre until Eden was claimed by the Fletchers. Elm arrived with food and stayed to support me when Brook left. By the time Kip returned after school, a few stragglers remained, but they didn't linger.

The fire had died, although the ashes still glowed. We left them to cool overnight.

As I turned the corner into School Lane, I began to believe in my new life. Ira was gone.

And Jay…?

What would happen when – if – Jay returned. Could our life continue as it had? Could we continue as we were?

Could I?

I didn't think so.

Jay's yearning for someone at the fair eclipsed anything I had ever sensed coming my way. Now I had experienced its intensity – albeit secondhand – I wanted nothing less from my partner.

It had seemed pointless trying to contact Jay again, so I didn't. Would lack of use weaken our connection? Or did it fade for other reasons as people grew further apart?

When did my familial bond with Ira die? Did we ever have one? If so, I didn't recall it.

Now, I had no-one but myself to answer to. I could do anything I wanted. At least, I could try.

A fledgling sense of freedom began to emerge. An exotic hatchling, it flexed its wings and felt its strength.

Fern's bark welcomed me as I opened the door to my cottage.

Day Thirteen, Jay

Shamed by our lazy lakeside day, we resolved to spend the next exploring. After a leisurely breakfast we were thinking of moving when a regular beat from downriver resolved into the high-pitched overhead whoosh of swans in flight. The pair landed neatly on our lake and floated serenely as their lofty gaze swept every ripple and verge.

Storm said, "That's all the view needed to make it perfect."

"Do you think they'll be here when we get back?"

"You're still thinking of going somewhere, then? The rate you're moving, it'll be time to get back before we're gone."

I threw a crust of bread, which Storm dodged. We eventually shifted ourselves and took to the road, following it in a roughly duskward direction. Along the way, I recounted the shiel-tale we told to small tarlings at bedtime…

…

"The star-born aren't created wise. The path to wisdom of a shiel or brownie can be as erratic as ours. When one misbehaves, it gets banished to earth and must earn its remission by helping the earthbound creatures. Every falling star you see in a clear night sky is another sheil falling to earth.

"And if you wish hard enough on a falling star, your wish might be heard and granted. Not always, 'cos it's hard for a brownie to hear with the wind in its ears, but if you're ever lucky enough to catch a falling star, its shiel is bound to grant only your wishes to earn its freedom. Stories are told about many who squandered their wishes and freed their brownie before they were sure what they truly wanted to wish for."

…

Storm declared it a pleasant fantasy, but everyone knew that shooting stars were the gods playing catch-ball.

I was deciding what song to begin when Storm suggested we speed up, but Swift wasn't built for speed, and I wasn't a seasoned rider. When pushed, it came out that Storm fancied we were being followed.

We couldn't be sure because trees hid the road behind us. It wasn't straight like a Tarn road. Storm wanted to continue our journey among the trees, out of sight of the road.

"I know I'm being anti-social, but we don't want to get caught up with someone looking for travelling companions to chatter to. And you can never be sure who it is on the road. It's better to be safe."

So, we rode into the woodland. It was cooler among the trees, although the leaves were already thinning to let through sunbeams. Storm set a brisk pace and kept checking behind us. When the path threatened to disappear, we led the horses till we came again to a river, probably the same river.

Storm's trap had provided for us the day before, but today we would fish for our dinner.

We collected wood, and I got a fire laid. At least that was one thing I was good at.

"Do you meet a lot of robbers on your Scarth roads?" I asked, half-joking.

"Not especially. Though if you're carrying valuables, you're better to travel with the Guardians touring the villages."

"Your Guardians don't only collect taxes and fine the villagers, then? It all sounds a bit oppressive compared to Tarn."

I knew little of how the other counties were regulated. I'd heard there was a new Minstrer's office in Tarn, set up to monitor compliance with the laws instead of merely issuing them, but that had only been running for a year or two.

"I don't know about Tarn, but I've seen no sign of any regulation at all in Seacrag. Half of it's only reached by boat, and some of the Seagan live in caves in the cliffs. The nearest thing to a village hall is the Drunken Sailor."

"Well, you could say the same about Fendle," I said. "Not that we live in caves, but the Barley Mow's where local business is done."

The world darkened as talk of Fendle reminded me. Tomorrow we must return to the fair and part soon afterwards.

"I've only been from Seacrag to Wendale," said Storm, "but there seems little enforcement of anything on this side of the Forest – certainly less than on our side. But then, your five counties together aren't much bigger than our region, so there's less to keep track of.

"The Wardens' Temple is in our neighbouring shire of Rawsten and it governs the shire beyond that. So, they have to be stronger than your Assemblies and Councils that only look after a county. There are more regions further shadeward, with their own authorities. Here, you've all got your own self-contained little territories, like going back in time. I love it!"

That was good to hear.

"Have you thought you might stay longer than the fair?"

I might be pushing my luck, but since the subject had come up…

My heartbeat paused for an answer. Storm smiled, a faint, five-candle smile, and brushed my hair from my eyes.

"Aw honey… Don't tempt me."

"Could I?"

Then my courage failed me. Before the pause could grow longer, I changed to another question that nagged at me.

"You could have your pick of anyone at the fair. Why choose me?"

"I didn't choose, love. You did. I wasn't looking. Now stop fishing! Come on, let's catch some fish we can eat."

So we did.

Or rather, Storm did.

I started the fire and found us mushrooms. Storm said they'd probably poison us, but I know a mushroom from a toadstool.

"I've been taught by an expert."

"Your Robin?"

"Not *my* Robin." I brushed aside the image of Robin that arose. "Trust me. These are good."

"My parents told me never to trust anyone who says, 'Trust me'."

By then, I was fully occupied, attempting to behead my fish without covering myself in evil-smelling guts. Storm took pity on me after neatly gutting and descaling one fish, and relieved me of the task.

"If you're left-handed, try doing it the other way around. I expect a right-handed person showed you. Don't sit next to me. Sit over there and imagine I'm you in a mirror. Then remember it that way next time."

I sat opposite, as instructed, but soon forgot to watch Storm's hands, beautifully mobile as they were. I preferred to watch the equally beautiful and mobile face.

Storm prattled on cheerfully.

"For someone who can make a good knife, you surely don't know how to use one. A fine knife's wasted on you. I could do a better job with one of your table knives. No, don't impale that one; you'll mangle it. You tend to the fire, and I'll skewer the fish."

Laughing at me, Storm's mind was no longer guarded, and it was only now I realised it had been closed to me all day. We'd been together, so it hadn't occurred to me.

"Something's been bothering you. You've not been with me since we left the road. Not properly."

Storm eyed me wordlessly for a moment.

"Our mind-link is strong, isn't it? They say that back before time, couples could truly share each other's thoughts, not just their feelings."

"Who says? Your Temple records?" Tarn history was all songs and stories.

"Maybe."

The knife paused in its cleaning of the fish.

"Sometimes you hear scraps from folk who've seen the records and come away remembering what they read – or what they think they read. Even the Wardens admit the records don't all make sense. There are strange symbols in them and unknown words, and records that refer to other records that've never been found."

It wasn't till later I remembered Storm hadn't answered my question.

The fish cooked quickly. I thought they'd still be raw, but my doubts were dismissed.

Afterwards, we stretched side by side on the riverbank. Storm conceded that we were still alive and pain-free.

"And the mushrooms were delicious."

"So was the fish; cooked to perfection."

"Not raw then? Good thing I didn't leave you in charge of the cooking."

It was true, I knew nothing about cooking. Or fishing. Not to mention the rabbit Storm had trapped, gutted, and skinned yesterday. My riding was, at best, pedestrian and I was still slow with the harness. Fingers that were nimble with etching and fine chains fumbled with thick leather and heavy buckles. Camping had been a romantic idea, but I hadn't considered the practicalities.

"I'm no bloody use for anything, am I?"

"Oh, I wouldn't say that, darlin."

We spent a pleasant afternoon discovering what I was good at, and at the time I thought nothing of it.

That evening, we were back at our lake later than expected. The swans had gone.

Storm was first to notice someone had been in our camp. Whoever it was hadn't tried to hide the fact. There were boot marks around and our things had been moved, but nothing was missing.

By this time, it was getting dark, and the wind had risen. When I'd brought the fire to a blaze, we sat under a blanket and watched the stars winking as clouds sped across them. Storm spoke then in a level voice. I had to concentrate to catch the words.

"I suspect that whoever's been rooting around our camp is the rider who followed us this morning. I think they've come from Scarth."

"From Scarth? Following you, you mean? But who? Why come all this way?"

"If it's who I think it is, they're after blood for killing one of theirs."

Day Thirteen, Robin

I was a dandelion seed freed from its stem. Fern picked up my mood and skipped around my feet as I hummed at the sink. The day passed lightly with no expectation of Ira to weigh it down or Jay to distract me, and the tarlings responded well to my buoyancy.

After feeding Fern and her brood, I walked to Cutler's Forge with barely a hitch in my step. Brook was cleaning bowls when I breezed into the kitchen.

"Can we bury Ira's ashes tomorrow afternoon? I'll need to be at school in the morning because Ty is taking the little ones seed-hunting."

"Of course we can. We'll meet you at the field, shall we?"

Kip appeared carrying bottles of cowslip wine. I asked if I could help with anything.

"Everything's under control, thanks. Go talk to Elm; dinner will be a while yet."

So I went to play spillikins with the older sprogs while Elm put the youngest to bed. When I returned, another guest had arrived and was helping to set the table.

"Hello, Robin. How are you?"

"Better. Thank you."

Eden nodded. "You seem more… reconciled. It must have been difficult not knowing. I'm sorry the outcome wasn't a happier one."

Over dinner, Kip and Brook led the conversation, and Eden's reserve thawed. By the time we were pouring cream over slabs of blackberry and apple pie, we'd dealt with the relative merits of Rowan's school and mine, and Kip comfortably raised a question that I hadn't dared venture.

"You seem young to be an Administrator, Eden."

"At the moment I am the youngest by a substantial margin. Not for much longer, though, if the Advisors get their way. They've been encouraging villages for years to select younger candidates as the posts fall vacant. Meanwhile, I go into work wondering if this will be the day someone sees through me and realises there's been a mistake. Then I'll find myself a messenger again, or even a thatcher."

"You didn't want to work with your family then?" Brook asked.

"There wasn't enough work to support us all. It's different now. Families are outgrowing their homes, tarlings are moving out to take up different lives, and people are building again, but there wasn't much demand ten summers ago."

I was doing sums in my head as Kip asked, "What did you do instead?"

"The Assemblies were looking for messengers, so I applied. It didn't pay well, but I had use of a horse whenever I wanted, which was handy as I'd just met Morgan, who lived outside Tarfen."

Neither Kip nor Brook queried the name, so Morgan must be Eden's partner.

Riding had not been a regular feature of my childhood. It was the only one of Ira's strictures I didn't challenge once I discovered how far away the ground was from the saddle. At least trees stayed put when you climbed them.

"Delivering messages doesn't sound a likely route into Assembly," Kip prompted.

"No, it was just luck that I was there at the right time. I knew my routes well and kept my eyes open, and I used to tell the Minstrers about anything on my routes that needed attention. Some even listened."

Kip topped up our beakers. Eden's unexceptional features had softened in the twofold haze of lamplight and cowslip wine.

"One time I mentioned to one of the Senior Administrators who did listen that I'd seen strangers hanging around the wealthy quarter who didn't look as if they lived there. Or worked there. Or worked anywhere, come to that. A couple of nights after that, some of the houses were broken into, so I was sent out with the warders to find the loiterers I'd seen."

"Surely they'd left the area?" Kip sounded surprised at such stupidity.

"They hadn't gone far. We found them still with most of their takings. After that, our friendly Minstrer, spoke to the Advisors, and they cleared us an office. I was installed in it to brief the messengers and co-ordinate whatever information they brought in. We've since taken on a couple of youngsters who patrol the town, and I was designated an Administrator so I have authority to call on the Assembly wardens if we need them. The Chief Warden wasn't too keen at first, but after a few well-received successes, they're happy to share the glory."

"Do you get a lot of theft then, in Tarfen?" Brook asked.

"Break-ins are happening more often. And attacks. Often, the thugs are coming together to plan their thefts. We don't get much of a budget. Some Minstrers disapprove of anyone younger than they are administering any budget at all."

"How old are you, Eden, if you don't mind me being nosy?" (*Good for Brook!*)

"Must be… thirty-one now. I lose track."

Brook smiled. "I know what you mean. I'm sure you're not allowed to lose track of Rowan's age, though. That's usually a good guide."

"That's true; Ro's forever reminding me that nine is almost grown up."

"Yes… I remember Jay was always in such a hurry to grow up. Wanted to catch up with Cris, I think." Brook's gaze shifted to the window. "It's a shame we can't let them know we've found Ira."

"Have you heard from Cris, at all?" I asked.

"We've had a message to say the horse cast a shoe and was being re-shod at Weffen, but we couldn't send one back there. They would have left before the pigeon arrived. The Loft hasn't any birds left for High Wenn now. The convoy's meant to be bringing some back."

"Pigeons aren't reliable, anyway." Said Eden. "It's not just the problem of predators. Unless you have a pre-arranged code, anyone might read your message. Can you imagine if you'd sent a pigeon instead of Cris and someone else read it and learned Jay was a suspect in someone's disappearance?"

My shiver must have been visible.

"Never mind, love," Brook's hand covered mine. "Cris will be there by now. Fair closes tomorrow. They'll be back soon enough, and we can put both their minds at rest."

I sensed Eden's eyes were on me, but when I raised my own, they were gazing at the darkened window. "Taz and I must go back soon, as well."

Brook started clearing the table and Kip told Eden about a Fletcher family event coming up in a few days.

"Taz won't want to miss the settling. Why don't you stay for that and go back together? You needn't go as Taz's guest; you could come as ours and escape with us if it goes on too long."

I'd have thought both Administrators perfectly capable of travelling alone, but Eden welcomed the proposal. Kip and Brook were pleased to have someone else to make a fuss of, in Cris's absence, but I doubted Morgan would be so happy with the delay. I started to help wash up but was told to sit and relax.

"Thanks, Brook, but I ought to get home to Fern. It's getting late."

I hoped that Eden would take the hint and leave, so that I could learn what else Kip and Brook knew, but my nudge misfired. Eden offered to walk me home, and Kip agreed on my behalf before I had time to decline gracefully.

Out in the yard, the stray terrier emerged from the stable and came to be stroked. He rolled onto his back as soon as Eden bent to pet him; it seemed a well-established routine. I half expected him to follow us, but the furry philanderer returned to his warm straw as we left the yard.

"Cute, isn't he?" said Eden.

"Fern obviously thought so. I'm less impressed with four crossbreed pups to find homes for."

"Would one get on with a cat, do you suppose?"

"That probably depends on the cat – at least, while it's a pup. If the cat isn't frightened of it, and if the pup doesn't chase the cat, they might get used to each other. You have a cat, then?"

"Ro does. If you think you'll have trouble finding homes for them… Are they old enough to leave yet?"

"Oh yes. They're weaned."

I suggested Eden spend more time with them before deciding. Since I would be off school next afternoon, we arranged a visit after I was back from burying Ira.

It would be worth an awkward hour or two, to find a home for another pup.

Day Fourteen, Jay

I woke early and alone.

I scrambled to my feet and must have looked as devastated as I felt, because Storm, who was already dressed, stopped saddling Blaze and hurried to where I stood drooping like yesterday's daisy-chain.

"Of course, I wouldn't leave without saying goodbye." Storm hugged me, but I pushed away, seeking eye contact and an explanation.

"I won't come back to the fair with you, Jay. I'll head for the mountain pass I came through with the Seagen and keep out of sight till they get there. The Devlins might think I've run away to Wendale or Tarn and give up searching. If not, I'll have to try to keep out of sight till we're back in Seacrag and hide in a cave till Sam can take me home."

The Devlins were the family looking for Storm.

"I won't hold you up anymore, Jay. The fair'll be packing up tomorrow. You'll be needed there."

Would I? I didn't think Storm sounded very certain, either.

"There isn't much left to pack up." Only what hadn't sold. I'd already loaded everything I'd bought, ready to go back with us to Fendle. The rest would be delivered.

"Won't they need Swift for the wagon?"

"They have another." Nobody brought wagons so far without spare horses. "On the other hand, you could run away to Tarn after all…"

Storm didn't answer but hugged me again. This time I clung like ivy. I didn't want to accept this was the end, and I sensed Storm had been as unprepared as I was.

"I don't suppose it would matter if I made my own way back to Fendle later," I said. "A horse travels faster than wagons; I might even catch up with the convoy."

Given my level of riding ability, we both knew this was unlikely. But there was nothing I did at the forge that somebody else couldn't pick up.

Storm held my shoulders when we moved apart and tried to look into my eyes, but mine were full and I didn't want to show it.

And Storm said, "Come with me then?"

As I raised them, the hope must have been easy to read.

"Just for today. If you're sure they can manage without you till tomorrow."

I'd decided they didn't need me then either. I'd briefed the youngsters on the goods to be delivered to Fendle, and Mikki had the paperwork.

"…But we need to go now."

So I packed my things, and we went.

We led the horses through the trees and heard the rustling of hooves on leaf-fall before we glimpsed a mount beyond the thinning clusters of undergrowth. Its solidly-built rider urged it towards the camp we had just left. We paused in silence until the hooves had passed out of hearing.

When we moved on, it seemed like ages passed before we reached the road where we could remount. We'd covered a good distance before we re-entered the cover of trees. After that, the horses picked their way more slowly on the rough tracks.

During the night, Storm had told me who the Devlins were, but little else. A clan of rogues, they came from a shire beyond Rawsten. On their home territory, they were hailed as protectors since they didn't prey on their neighbours. In other shires, their presence heralded thefts and disappearances. Nothing had been proved against them in Rawsten's district. Accusers were liable to retract their accusations or, occasionally, to disappear.

There was no singing that day. We had little opportunity to talk either, as we threaded our way through woodland alongside the road that led to the Llannoc pass. It was slow going.

Towards evening we came to an inn. We watched from the cover of trees long enough to satisfy Storm that no-one was behind us and it might be safe to take a room.

In the warmth of our seclusion, we ate a civilised mutton pie and relaxed at last. Lying where we'd collapsed on the bed, Storm turned to me.

"You needn't come further if you should get back to the fair."

I registered that "if".

"I don't have to. What will you do if this Devlin character follows the Seagen convoy?"

"I have to return Blaze. I might be able to hide in the wagons. It's safer in a crowd. In Seacrag, it'll be easy to stay out of sight till we leave. I'll be safe once I'm in Scarth with my family and the Guardians about. I wonder how a Devlin got over here."

"Did you really kill one of them?"

"I threw the knife, so I was the cause. They were raiding our horses. We knew they'd been seen heading Scarth-wards from a horse fair in Rawsten we'd been to, so we were stabling as many as we could at night and keeping the rest close to the house.

"The night they came, the dogs gave us warning. There were three of them ready to make off with our horses; but they'd had to break the gate to open it and they'd been greedy, trying to round up all of them. It had all taken them too long. I'm good with a throwing knife," –there was no pride in the claim, just a statement of fact– "so I aimed at the shoulder of the front rider, thinking it'd hold up the ones behind and my sibs'd get a chance at them. The kid fell off and was trampled by the horses."

Storm took a deep breath. "The other two just rode off and left 'n. The poor beggar can't have been more than sixteen or seventeen summers. Took half the night to die." I shared the shadow of Storm's memory. "The healer we fetched couldn't do anything."

"Didn't they come back?"

"Next day they sent a go-between to demand back their 'kidnapped' youngster. They got a body. We'd called in the local Guardians by then. They'd seen the state of the body and the empty paddock and the damage. They know us. We sell them their mounts."

Eyes met mine as if waking from a nightmare.

"After that, the Devlins vanished like stars at sunrise. We knew they'd be back, but I didn't think they'd go to these lengths to get at me."

"How long ago was it?"

"Last winter, but they've long memories. They want blood for blood."

We pursued our own thoughts until I ended the silence.

"I'm coming with you. You don't know the territory."

Neither did I. It didn't occur to me I'd be more hindrance than help to an accomplished rider trying to stay out of sight. Storm must have thought it but didn't say so.

"They'll need you back at the fair, Jay."

I said, "Will you take some money then for food, and a bed when it rains?"

We'd argued over this before, so I was confident of the answer.

"You know I won't. You need it yourself."

"Then I'm coming with you."

The dark frown persisted, but the echoes that reached me of Storm's troubled feelings revealed, I thought, a different preference.

I hadn't forgotten my family's debt. Less money than I'd hoped was returning to Fendle and there would be one less worker to complete the tavern's order. But it wouldn't be for long.

It had lodged in my mind that Storm might still be persuaded to come with me to Tarn. Even if persuasion took until Llannoc or Seacrag, or even Scarth… didn't I want to see the world?

Through the afternoon, Storm raised more objections but, to me, they sounded half-hearted. That evening I mustered the keenest weapons in my armoury to overcome the last shreds of resistance. Before we slept, I was rewarded with a murmur close to my ear.

"Stuff it, then. Come with me."

Day Fourteen, Robin

Kip and Brook helped me with Ira's grave.

Redbreasts watched us dig, waiting for worms to appear. Sal and Aspen's remains were here somewhere, but their location was unimportant. If funeral smoke had truly borne Ira's spirit to the shades, they would reunite there, not underneath four ells of riverside dirt. A chill wind blew my hair into my eyes and made them water.

The finished mound looked bleak and barren, but grass and wildflowers would cover it soon enough. I scattered seeds of lavender and herbs harvested from our plot at the cottage, to flower among the grasses.

Kip and Brook had confirmed they wanted a pup but were happy to forgo first pick. The afternoon was already darkening when Eden knocked at my door.

It was easier to tell the pups apart now their personalities were developing. I drew attention to each pup's good points as I handed them over to be examined and petted. Then we sat with a cup of Brook's raspberry wine, watching them play together.

The conversation turned from pups to poisons. Eden wanted to know which plants were poisonous, where they grew, and what other plants they resembled.

I was halfway through Fendle's most common plants when Eden said, "I'll never remember so many, and I need to see them to be sure? Did you never want to be an apothecary, like your parents?"

"I'd assumed I would until Taz offered me the school. They asked Kip first and Kip suggested me for the job. Did you know Kip was a teacher before settling with Brook? It made more sense for Kip to come to Fendle than for Brook to seek work at Tarlake."

"You had no teaching experience?"

"No, but neither had anyone else in Fendle, and at least I had Kip. The teacher in post was about to settle with someone in Hunsden. Taz probably thought me a good long-term bet, being unlikely to settle and move out of Fendle."

Eden's immediate response checked at the first syllable. I had the impression the next question was a forced return to script after resisting a digression.

"Do you enjoy teaching?"

"Most of the time. The biggest attraction was getting out of the house every day. Does that sound terrible? Ira wasn't the easiest person to live with. The cottage was a bonus, of course, but if I'd spent my days here, like a hermit, mixing up lotions and potions, I think Ira would have sent me crazy. School was the best part of the day." Except for the times spent with Jay, but I didn't say it. "I have Kip and Taz to thank for my job and my sanity."

Eden's eyebrows drew together in thought.

"How were Taz and Jess chosen?"

"How are any Administrators chosen? I'd have been at school back then."

"It depends on the village. Procedures differ. Some get voted in, but most of the older Minstrers came from prominent families who wanted to increase their influence.

Certain villages are known to have 'elevated' their busybodies to Assembly to get them out of the way."

"That would fit Jess nicely: meddling in everyone's business and always knowing best."

"Maybe. It would have suited Jess's interests, too. Tarfen's a bigger cow to milk. Don't underestimate Jess Giltin."

"The Giltins still have a house here, but none of them seem to live in it. Jess's partner's been dead two or three years and their youngsters spend more time in Tarfen than Fendle."

"That'll be the Mucky Duck. The Giltins have been running the tavern for the past couple of summers, and it's taken a lot of custom from the Blue Shiel. The Duck was well-appointed from the start, with every inducement to attract customers. An Administrator's salary is generous, but I wouldn't have thought it enough to set up your children in business."

We were interrupted by one of the bitch pups, who jumped at my leg, yipping to be noticed. A grey-fawn brindle with white markings, she was more forward than the others. I lifted her and Eden took her from me.

"I can see you want all the attention. Rowan would love you. Can I take this one home with me?"

"You're welcome. What will you call her?"

"I'll probably leave that to Ro."

"What's your cat called?"

"Erm... Puss." Eden shrugged.

I suggested Eden visit the pup before they left for Tarfen in the hope that better acquaintance might inspire a name. The key to the cottage could be collected from me in school at any time.

After Eden left, I sat as the pups played. Soon they be off to new homes.

"Then it'll be just you and me, Fern."

I promised I would set about finding homes for the other two tomorrow. She watched my face as I spoke to her.

"You'll miss them when they're gone," I said. She came and put a paw on my knee. "I'll probably miss them more than you will. They might all be gone before the convoy's back."

I wouldn't let it soften me. No pining, no regrets. Not for the pups. Not for anyone.

I counted the days.

Today was the last day of the fair. They'd be packing up tomorrow and travelling the day after – five or six days' journey. I hoped my resolve would stay firm when the time came.

Day Fifteen

Jay

Our destination was the inn called the World's End, on Wendale's border at the foot of the Llannoc mountains. We didn't plan to stay at the inn itself but to rest out of sight for a day or two and wait for the Seagen convoy. There was no cover for us in the pass if we tried to travel through it alone.

We looked forward to that rest. I wasn't used to riding so far, and Storm was worn from the strain of watching behind us.

My thoughts were hazy as the morning's mist, but not so cool. The forge didn't need me. Elm made knives as good as mine. No-one but me saw a future in armlets, necklets, and earrings. I'd yet to grow my market and Fendle wasn't the most fertile ground for it.

The thought of travelling back to the fair alone brought an empty ache where Storm had become lodged. Was Storm my new future? I needed more time to find out.

My head might be cloudy, but my heart's preference was crystal clear. I'd bring it to Storm when we could stop and rest and talk properly.

We kept to the woodland as much as possible. Where paths were rutted or overgrown, we dismounted and led the horses. Swift was unsure on the uneven ground, but Storm spoke calmly to soothe him. I recognised the same patient tone that had been used to reason with me the previous day.

There'd been no sign of a follower since the lake. Certain that I would feel safer on a firmer track, I persuaded Storm we should take the road for a faster ride. Once this was agreed, I directed Swift to a break in the trees where the ground levelled to the road. It would be quicker than waiting till the path met the road further on.

The ground was level enough, but as we passed a ridge of rough grass, a ground-bird rose squawking from the cover, causing Swift to lurch. My seat shifted. Wanting something more solid than reins, I clung to the horse's neck as he shot forward to the road.

Storm quickly reached us, stopped Swift and was calming him while I hung on grimly with all four limbs to halt my sideways slide. The danger had passed, and although my inclination was to keep hanging on, which had worked for me so far, I mustered my most nonchalant expression, denied my thumping heartbeats, and raised myself to a sitting position.

I'd slipped further than I realised. My right foot was free of the stirrup and smoothly, inevitably, I slid sideways in a graceful arc…

Things became less graceful as I clutched vainly at Swift's neck again. My left foot was still in the twisted stirrup, and I found myself suspended by it, upside down. Storm was still talking quietly to Swift, trying not to laugh.

All would have been well had I not fallen so clumsily when my foot suddenly slipped free. I rolled blindly and flung out my hands to stop myself. Swift, still listening to Storm, stepped politely sideways away from my body and on to my right hand.

Every sense registered white screaming pain. The smell of blood mingled with the taste of bile. As hearing returned, I heard a low keening punctuated by curses. As thought returned, I realised the sobbing was mine.

My eyes opened on darkness before focusing on the dirt beneath my hunched body. My whole being was curled around my screaming hand.

I made no sense of Storm's voice and rolled onto my back. The face above me registered helpless distress, so I forced myself to sit and inspect the agony.

The blood was more than a few narrow fingers should've held. I flexed the thumb, which was unharmed. The next finger looked untouched, but waves of pain met any attempt to move it. I had to deal with it quickly – Robin had taught me that much – but concentrating was an effort.

"Water. I need water and something to pour it into."

We'd brought plenty from the lake, not knowing when we'd find more. We had boiled it last night. I filled the bowl Storm brought from a saddlebag and submerged my fingers. The water brought temporary relief. It was quickly clouded by crimson swirls drifting from my wounds.

I lifted my damaged hand with the other and rested it on my leg. With my good hand, I emptied the bowl and filled it with fresh water before returning my throbbing hand. Now I saw the damage. Three fingers lay in unnatural positions, still oozing threads of blood. Patches of skin had been scraped away, and the outer part of my hand looked unnaturally flat. I must keep it clean, or the wounds would blacken, and I might lose my hand, or my arm. Or my life, so Ira had warned over our scrapes and skinned knees.

I'd have given anything then for Robin's lotions and potions and practical common-sense. Storm hovered, helpless, above me.

"I'm going to need something clean to bandage this with."

Given at last something useful to do, Storm went to raid our saddlebags.

"And something to dry my hand."

The throbbing echoed through me. What did Robin recommend for pain?

I scanned the woodland verge where Blaze and Swift calmly grazed the rough grass but could identify nothing useful. Nor was there anything flat and firm to bind my fingers against to hold them flat. Storm searched the undergrowth, but eventually we settled for binding my fingers tightly together to immobilise the crushed bones.

Straightening the hand and pulling the fingers together was a painful business and started the wounds bleeding again. Storm stopped whenever I cried out, so I tried not to, biting down on a leather strap and holding the fingers straight with my other hand while Storm bound them. The pain blurred into a single red mist to fill the world.

I had used most of our water and we needed more, but I was in no state to go searching. Storm went to find more after clearing a hollow for me in some undergrowth where I could rest unseen. I was glad by then to be alone to whimper, and drifted in and out of sleep, only to be woken again by the throbbing of my hand and arm. It had been swelling as we bandaged, and I told myself it was natural for bruising to spread. Pain peaked in waves. When it subsided, I drifted towards sleep, only to be woken by the next wave.

Would I be able to work again at my craft? Or my delicate jewellery? And what of my lute? How could I work with one good hand? It was too much to think about.

My left hand rose to rub at my silver earring, but it was gone – lost in the fall. The other was still in place. I'd have to wear one for now, like Robin.

Perhaps that was something I could do – teach?

I struggled to imagine myself in front of a classroom.

My thoughts veered from Fendle to more recent events. When I'd howled with the pain, Storm had suffered too. I'd had to argue my need for more water or Storm wouldn't leave me.

How would I face my family now?

My circling thoughts settled on the night before, when Storm had said, "Come with me." Was that my future now? Whatever I needed to learn, to adapt, I'd do it somehow. I wouldn't become anyone's burden.

Robin

Kip decided to take the other bitch puppy, so I had two dogs left to find homes for. I told my class the pups were ready to leave their mother and emphasised that they were crossbreeds. I made it clear I would need to talk to their parents first and there was no point anybody asking for a pup until I had their parents' agreement.

At least five hands shot up anyway to claim a puppy. There may have been more. I was badly in need of a haircut and kept tossing it out of the way to see who I was talking to.

141

If all the parents asked agreed to take one, I had no idea how I'd decide who was to get them.

Fin's eyes didn't leave me. I only wish my lessons had received as much attention. It was unnaturally quiet in that corner since I'd been back at school. Kip had worked wonders.

Later, Fin came to ask me if I knew who sired the pups.

"He's a little tan-and-white terrier. You've probably seen him hanging around the forge."

"They'd be no use for hunting then?"

"For rats and mice, maybe. They won't run as fast as a hound. Their legs will be shorter. I expect they'll dig, but they may grow too big to put down a rabbit hole. It's difficult to tell for sure until they're grown."

Fin nodded and wandered off, barely pausing to snap at something Cay said as they passed each other. Those two rarely spoke now, and Fin walked home alone.

That afternoon, a sudden shock of Jay invaded my thoughts – not a tentative seeking, but a blaze of pain. I couldn't concentrate on what I'd planned and gave the class something to do that didn't need my input.

Jay's pain was a physical one, I could tell that much, but infused with uncertainty and confusion, like a child wanting comfort. The feeling would fade and later stir again to jar me. It came again during the night but fainter, as if control was returning. By morning, it was gone.

Day Seventeen

Jay

The next two days were a blur of pain, and road, and trees, and sky, and more pain.

I'd used my undershirt to fashion a sling for travelling and hoped the weather wouldn't turn colder. When a stumble jogged my hand, the pain that shot through me made me gasp and gripped my stomach so that I struggled to keep any food I might have forced down. Afterwards, the arm throbbed for ages. Sometimes the fingers tried to flex in automatic response to some movement of the horse, and that was a new agony.

We planned to camp near the inn called the World's End, below the mountain, but progress on the road was slow. Storm fretted about how ill I looked, which did nothing to make me feel better. When we reached the Blasted Oak, which was the last inn before the World's End, Storm insisted we stop there instead and take a room.

Should I send a message back to Fendle to tell my family where I was? Was there a village nearby? I didn't know myself what I would do next; what could I tell them?

In our room, we unwrapped my hand again to change the dressing. Storm shredded what remained of my second shirt and salvaged enough to re-bind the fingers before washing and drying the soiled dressing. The bruises on my hand and my swollen wrist were turning yellow, but the stripped flesh was drying. I thought it looked clean.

"I can move my thumb." Although the surrounding swelling reduced its range. I gritted my teeth and tried moving the index finger, then swallowed the gasp that wanted to escape. "I can't move that yet – not without hurting the others. But I think it's whole. That's something then. I've a thumb and forefinger."

Would a thumb and forefinger have the power to hold metal for shaping? Would one good hand offer enough dexterity for the delicate silverwork that had become my retreat and relaxation? Not for the first time, I thanked the shiel that it was my right hand I had damaged.

Storm raided the firebox on our way in and found a flat fragment of broken furniture destined for the fire. It was thin, and easy to trim into splints. We wrapped them in the clean strips and bound them tightly either side of my broken fingers. As well as immobilising the hand and protecting it, the splints reminded me not to try using it. If the fingers mended straight, they might not appear too deformed, but I didn't expect them to move again unaided. The bones under the bruises didn't look right.

We decided we would wait for the convoy at the Blasted Oak instead of going on to the World's End. We were on the Llannoc road so the Seagen must pass us. And it was a less obvious meeting place than the World's End if our stalker should be waiting there for the convoy. Storm could hide in a wagon before then.

We were early to bed. Storm lay snuggled behind with an arm across me, careful not to disturb my hand. I stroked the sheltering arm, already half asleep. This wasn't how I'd imagined us filling our wait for the convoy.

"Never mind," I murmured. "We can make up for lost time later."

Storm gurgled behind me.

"Oh, yes? I can imagine us in the throes of passion, and you give out one of your shot-hare screams. Apart from spoiling the moment, we'd have the innkeeper up here crying murder."

I chuckled too. "I meant after. The hand'll hurt less in a couple of days."

"In a couple of days, love, the Seagen will have arrived, and I'll be gone."

I didn't reply as I processed this.

Storm sensed something was wrong and said, as if in consolation, "Let's see how things are tomorrow."

"I thought I was coming with you."

"Oh Jay, that would be good. But I can't expect you to come across the mountains with us. How would you get back again, with that hand and no-one to help? In fact, I think you should stay longer here before you try to travel again."

"Come with me" didn't mean to Scarth, then.

I hadn't probed at the time because I didn't think that was what I wanted. Knowing it wasn't on offer convinced me that it was what I wanted.

"I'd been thinking of maybe coming with you further than that."

Feeling my disappointment, but misreading its cause, Storm was solicitous and said again, "See how you feel tomorrow."

I knew how I would feel tomorrow. And the day after that. Storm didn't feel the same, or we'd have spoken before of our options for staying together, if only to dismiss them. It seemed Storm hadn't even considered the possibility.

Was there more that I hadn't been told? I resolved to discover what Storm was keeping from me.

Robin

Fin wasn't at school. I thought nothing of it; Fin often took a day to go hunting.

In the past, I'd welcome the respite. Before their rift, Cay would go too but, instead, was today sulking in the classroom. Not because of Fin's absence, but because the Elvers refused to take a puppy.

Not far into the first lesson, Vern Hartwood arrived to report that Fin had taken off overnight. Food was missing from their pantry, and a hunting knife was gone. The disappearance of other items over past weeks was now explained. This was no sudden impulse. The outraged parent demanded to know if Cay, or any of the class, knew where Fin might be.

The Hartwoods were known to be harsh parents, and the interrogation bore this out. Cay suffered the worst of it and began to stammer, which further aggravated Vern.

I called a halt, promising to inform the family if I learned more. My intervention earned me abuse and thinly veiled accusations of sorcery. I was charged with perverting tarlings – specifically, Fin – and was unfit to teach. I had been overheard consulting with my familiars by people passing the cottage.

Eventually Vern Hartwood left. After the door slammed, the room was silent. Cay was shaking and many of the younger ones were upset. I tried to sound calm and sympathetic as I explained that Parent Hartwood was worried for Fin and so was upset. The class was subdued for the rest of the morning, but after Vern's accusations, I couldn't be sure which of us they were more frightened of.

When we broke for lunch, I spoke to Cay alone. It seems Fin often talked of running away from parents who expected their children would work in their stead to feed the family as soon as they left school. And from a village that had already judged any young Hartwood.

Cay – perhaps less exploited by the Elvers – never showed courage enough to leave the village, so had been told no more of Fin's intentions. Could that be why their friendship foundered?

In the afternoon, Eden came to collect the cottage key but instead stayed to talk to the tarlings. They wanted to know more about this new department that searched for troublemakers and missing people. Was that just in Tarfen, or all of Tarn? Did that include Fin?

"Fin… is that the tall, moody one?

"Yes, that's the one. Not much of a troublemaker now, though, according to Kip."

"The evidence suggests that Fin ran away, so that wouldn't be a case for us. We'd look for someone we had reason to believe had been kidnapped or injured."

Tarfen's troublemakers were a welcome distraction from the morning's drama. Eden avoided being drawn into the grislier details that might trigger nightmares in the younger ones, but the blood-thirst of twelve or thirteen summers heard enough to feed the imagination. Some of the Assembly's messengers weren't much older.

"Do you need messengers for Fendle?"

"Messengers go out on Assembly business, so they're based in Tarfen, where Assembly sits. They only deliver other messages if the recipients are on their official route.

It *would* be good to have messengers for the villages, but pigeons are cheaper. They work for bird-feed."

"But if there was a messenger in each village, you'd know who was there and what was happening."

"We use information from the messengers who are already out there, but if we wanted to appoint lookouts in each village, that would be a different job. We'd need to find a new name for them."

The class spent the rest of the afternoon thinking up names for this potential role, not all complimentary. I wondered if we might get them thinking of names for Rowan's puppy, but it was time to go home before I could suggest it.

While I tidied up, some of the younger 'lings came to talk to Eden. They would be a similar age to Rowan, who I envisaged as tall for nine, pale, hawk-like, and serious. I had no information to support this. Ro might take after Morgan and be altogether different.

On the way home, we collected fresh bracken for the dogs' bedding.

I would reinstate Fern's old blanket when the pups were gone, but since the whelping, I'd used bracken and replaced it daily. After sweeping out her corner, I made us tea while Eden played with whatshername and her siblings.

Just two families had agreed to take a pup, sparing me a decision that might have upset someone, so now all had homes to go to. They ought to go soon before anyone changed their mind.

I poured our tea, almost missing the cups as my hair got in the way. I should tackle it before tomorrow's settling ceremony, or I'd be flinging my petals at the wrong couple.

When Eden left, I found the shears and peered into the polished mirror hanging over my drawer chest. Ira had always trimmed my hair and never let it reach an unmanageable length. It had never been this shaggy. I liked it longer, but I still needed to see where I was going. Tucking the sides behind my ears, I hacked at what now hung over my face.

I could see again, but I couldn't honestly call it an improvement. I started to trim the line straighter but became distracted by pups playing with the clippings on the floor. At least now I could see properly to sweep them up. As I did so, it became clear that clippings had found their way under my clothing.

Afterwards, when I looked again in the mirror, the fringe appeared less uneven than before. The effect was still brutal, but I feared that further cropping would make it more so.

I put the shears in a drawer before the temptation to snip became stronger, and I went to bed. All night I was itching.

Day Eighteen, Jay

After a full day's rest, I felt better, and made sure to say so. Once settled in its sling, the throbbing in my hand had receded to a background ache, so long as I didn't try to move it.

No rider had turned up looking for us. The wagons from the fair hadn't arrived yet, and by now they would have made camp for the night, somewhere else. I prepared to honour our last evening together.

I spent my remaining funds on the strongest ale and cider the Blasted Oak could provide. It was delivered to our room while Storm was away checking on the horses and I distributed it in discrete, easy-to-retrieve locations, so its abundance was less obvious. I sensed Storm was returning before I'd finished hiding them all, but some flasks could be left in view.

We ate in our room, side-by-side on the bed, leaning together with our backs against the wall and our barley wine on a chair beside me. I kept Storm's topped up and started with a safe topic.

"Samphire owes you the fair this season. Most of their customers came to the stall to hear more about you. I don't think the Seagen bought their own drinks the whole week."

"Fair enough for them. They got me out of a tight spot. And took me to the fair to boot, where I met you, my love."

Storm lifted a toast to me, and we touched beakers. I topped up our drinks. Storm, being already fairly relaxed, didn't notice that I added less to mine.

"What was it like in the Shade Forest? Sam said you were looking for a horse in there."

"In a manner of speaking. I was trying to find my way back to where I'd left her. She wasn't far in, so I'm hoping she found her way home. You can't take a horse far into the Border Forest."

"Why try? What were you doing there?"

Storm loved nothing so much as telling a story.

"The Devlins were after me. I'd been looking for harness on the cheap at a local saddler's who was selling up, when a couple of Devlins turned up at the sale. I thought I'd got out without them seeing me, but there was another waiting outside. So I bolted.

"There'd been a terrible storm brewing. The wind was howling like the banshee, and the Devlins were howling to match, so I made for the Forest – just to hide under cover for a bit. I rode the horse in as far as I could and then left her and dived into the thick of it. Only, when I stopped running, I couldn't find the way back. I'd hacked and torn my way in and pulled branches across to hide my path. You'd have thought when I turned 'round I'd see where I came through, but I swear it'd grown over again in the time it took me.

"I was wandering for ages. It felt like days, though it might have been only the one night. I didn't dare sleep for the noises around me. My knife was to hand the whole time. I'd no food or water, except for the rain. When I came to water, it was salty so I couldn't drink it. And that's where the Seagen found me. They'd pulled in to make good their sail and they took pity on me. You'll have heard about that from Samphire."

After a long draught of ale – storytelling was thirsty work – I topped up the drinks again. Storm kissed my neck, and we spend an idle ten minutes saying little.

Storm spoke first. "I'm go'n to miss yer so much… You do know how I feel about you?"

I captured Storm's misted eyes as best I could.

"You don't have to miss me, you know. I could come with you if you wanted me to. I could come all the way with you."

"Darlin you can go all the way with me any time."

Storm was relaxed as a brewery rat. I was bleary myself but not drunk enough to be diverted so easily from my purpose. I reached behind the bed for a fresh flask and somehow fixed it steady between right arm and thigh while my good hand removed the stopper. Storm watched the ale fill the beaker as I spoke.

"There's something you're not telling me, isn't there? Did you think I couldn't tell? Does it matter now if I know if we're not going to see each other again?"

"Don't say that, love. It sounds so…"

Storm's eyes were brimming. They looked sincere, but that would be the barley wine.

"Why don't I come with you, then?"

Storm tried to focus; I'd pierced the haze.

"You can't do that, love."

"Tell me, then. What are you so worried about? Why would the Devlins follow you so far?"

"Not all of 'em." The tone was grim. The words trailed off and Storm's eyes closed. "I didn't realise they'd go so far. 'S what worries me… my family is there without me."

I thought that was all I was going to get until Storm started up again, slurred but understandable. "My scarlings… if they can't get to me…"

"Scarlings?"

Storm's head shook like a dog's as if to shake off the drink.

"Willow 'n' Bracken."

I allowed this to sink in.

"You have children. Then you have a partner. You're settled."

There was an inevitability to it. The two scarlings were an added refinement, but that wasn't what hurt most.

"Yes. Well… yes." Another gap was clearing in the haze. "I was young, y'see? We soon knew it wasn' workin. But then there was Willow."

Storm slid a little further down the wall.

" 'N Paddi dun't have any family but mine."

I took a deep breath, but it juddered in my throat.

"Storm. Storm, don't go to sleep." My head was suddenly clear. I shook the wilting shoulders until they braced and then distanced myself on the bed.

"So, you've been settled for… years."

Storm nodded, eyes on mine. I steadied my voice.

"And you have two 'lings." I poured myself a full drink.

"They're why I mus go home, you see? Not Paddi."

"And while I was falling for you, head over heels, you didn't think to mention this? You couldn't tell me you had scarlings and a partner at home? Right at the start? Did Samphire know?"

"It didn' come up. Jay, I wasn't expecting… you." I shook my head in disbelief. "Honest, Jay. I didn't think anythin would come of it. And then, when it did…"

"If you'd told me at the start, nothing *would've* come of it!"

Wouldn't it?

Would I have moved on? Looked elsewhere? At least I'd have known what to expect. I'd have held something back. "I suppose you thought you might as well have some fun while you were away from home."

I'd hit a nerve. Storm's eyes flashed. "And, of course, you came to the fair looking for a meaningful relationship with nobody waiting for you back home! Come on, love, you practically ate me alive back when I was trying to be friends. Don't try to make out it was *me* wanting my wicked way. Gods, Jay! For someone who's so keen to canter, you're a bloody prig."

The music was gone from Storm's voice. Hands covered those wounded eyes, rubbing to erase the sight of me.

I scrambled off the bed, forgetting my damaged wrist, which screamed protest. But I had to put distance between myself and this body that, damn it, I still wanted. This should have been our last night making memories.

I stuffed an unopened flask of cider in my saddlebag with my good hand and tucked another of barley wine under my right arm. Everything took too long. I couldn't get away fast enough.

Storm protested. "Oh, come on, Jay; don't throw your toys out of the crib!"

Stung by the scorn, I dropped the barley wine in my haste to escape Storm's disdain. I tried catching it as it fell and hurt my hand again. Hot with pain and frustration, I snatched up another bottle and stuffed it beside the one in my saddlebag.

This time, Storm's voice was weary, resigned.

"Look, you have the room. I'll sleep downstairs, in the parlour."

It only strengthened my resolve. I reached the door.

"Jay, stop. Be sensible!"

Furious with myself, I put down the bag to open the door with my good hand.

"Come on, Jay. Don't let's end like this."

The door started to swing shut again. I held it open with my foot while I stretched to pick up the bag again. Storm belatedly scrambled off the bed and was hampered by the fallen cover as I made it through the door.

"Please, love, don't go yet. Just lie down for a while, till you feel stronger. Think about it. Just for a little while."

I closed my ears. My parting shot will have carried to every customer in the Blasted Oak.

"Just stop it. Shut up! I'm not listening. Don't follow me. I don't want to see you again."

Shiel knows how I managed to carry the bag with me without spilling anything, all the way downstairs and outside, and across the road to the woodland. Both flasks were intact when I collapsed under the trees, and both were empty when I woke in the morning.

Day Eighteen, Robin

It was Funday: the week's end after six days of work.

In the past, teaching hadn't felt so much like work. I had spent too long at home.

Eden arrived dressed for the occasion in deep sapphire with matching blue stone ear-studs. We had puppy-time in hand before we were due at the forge to walk together to the settling celebrations.

When I opened the door, Eden's eyes went to the newly trimmed fringe and blinked. I sensed a quickly shielded reaction. Until then I hadn't thought us attuned in any way.

"You've cut your hair."

"I know." Eden wasn't normally one to state the obvious.

I relented. "I needed to see where I was going. But it looks wrong, doesn't it? I ought to cut it all."

"No! No, don't do that. Will you let me just trim a bit? I've had practice. I cut Ro's."

It couldn't be much worse than it looked now, so I fetched the shears. Eden found a cover for my shoulders, which I should have thought of yesterday. I sat on the high stool, trying not to appear worried. I couldn't decide where to look, so I closed my eyes as the snipping began.

"Joy! Shears that cut."

They were Jay's blades: lighter than Elm's and good for shearing. It reassured me that Eden wasn't chopping off great chunks. The sharp tip of the shears pecked at the ends of my fringe, like a bird pecks at seed. When the fringe was deemed satisfactory, the shears began to peck elsewhere around my head, finishing up at my hacked ends.

Fingers ran through my hair to release the loose cuttings. It sent a shiver through me from head to heels. This must be how a cat feels when stroked.

Footsteps circled to pause in front of me, and I opened one eye to view the reaction. Eden's met mine and winked. I would have been less surprised if one of the animals carved in the fireplace winked at me. I blinked and Eden's eyes had returned to my hair. After performing more snips with a theatrical flourish, the artist stood back and nodded approval.

"Go see what you think. I can take off more if you want, but I think it suits you at that length."

At the mirror I could hardly believe the improvement. My hair was no shorter but seemed lighter, and the blunt fringe had softened. It had something of my former shagginess, but somehow more controlled. I shook my head, and it all fell back into place. I had a hairstyle, not just a mop.

"Thank you. That is amazing! I am impressed. Where did you learn to do that?"

"I learned from my mistakes; Ro was fortunately too young to notice at the time. Nowadays I'd be scolded for any hair out of line. Is it time we went?"

I retrieved the silver earrings Jay had given me before leaving. Committed now to transformation, I wore them both.

Eden blinked. "They're different."

"Asymmetric, like me."

An oak chest against the wall held clothing from happier days, which Ira never threw out, although none were ever worn again. Wafts of elm, bay and lavender met me as I delved into its depths. Each garment had been shaken every year and refolded.

I half expected to hear a spectral moan threatening reprisal for my violation, but I persevered and found what I sought – a rich purple cloak to set off my mushroom-toned suit. Eden nodded approval. It was useful to have a disinterested friend to advise me.

Not everyone troubled with a settling ceremony now, but the Fletchers loved to host an event.

The happy couple planned to continue working with their own families, so neither were changing their name as Kip had when moving here to settle with Brook. The pair still wore traditional undyed fabric, though, to symbolise the fresh start together in a new life. I'd heard that in past times, one might have worn a blue cowl and the other red, and some of the oldest songs referred to this custom. There was disagreement about its significance. Cowls were out of fashion now.

The barn was festive with the usual cacophony of colour. The centre had been cleared for dancing, and straw bales set around the outside for seating. Tarnfolk clustered behind the doors or around the barrel of ale with its neighbouring trestle that bore jugs of sloe and cowslip wine. Another trestle bore food. Tarlings chasing around the straw bales swooped on it when they thought nobody was watching, to carry off a sugared berry.

Outside, the villagers who weren't invited to the party gathered to wish the couple good luck and were offered a drink for their good wishes. A second barrel had been set outside, where well-wishers could collect their customary refreshment and enjoy the music echoing into the night air.

We sat with the Naismiths. This was Elm's family, distant cousins to the Cutlers and Wysmiths. The musicians settled with their drinks at one end of the barn and gentle background strains mingled with the chatting and laughing and occasional shrieks of tarlings. Two singers I didn't recognise joined the players while we ate. Their singing was indifferent, but the shorter of them clowned around and made the tarlings laugh, so I resolved to add my coins to the hat when it came around. When a louder chord heralded a familiar tune, all eyes turned to the middle of the barn.

The newly settled pair led the dancing and after a decent interval, other couples joined them, slowly circling to the familiar tune. The music changed to a galloping rhythm, and the dance changed to match. More couples joined in, followed by a joyous trail of Fletcher tarlings who disrupted the sets but were tolerated, because it was a celebration and nobody was drunk yet.

Eden turned to me with hands open and we joined the confusion. I don't dance often, but the settling dance is an easy one for tarlings to join in and I can manage it without tripping over my feet.

Back at our bales, one of the Fletchers claimed Eden and Kip tried to persuade me out to dance, but the reel was more complex, so I declined. If my limp let me down, I would upset the pattern for the others. Kip partnered Elm instead. The players stamped their feet to encourage the guests to clap to the rhythm, and the dance space filled.

When the musicians took their break, the singers took over. This time, their simple unaccompanied harmonies were more successful. When the dancing resumed, the singers toured the barn for contributions before joining the well-wishers outside.

Eden offered a hand to join the dancing, so hesitantly that I didn't like to snub the request. Fortunately, musicians play more of the simple dances at settlings to encourage children to join in.

It was soon after that the noise outdoors grew louder than the music, and people burst in shouting that the Tillers' barn was on fire. It was across the next field, and most of the guests ran to help. A few stayed to keep the tarlings together and watched the flames from outside.

I was one of the last to join the chain passing water from the river. The burning bales of hay had been dragged out of the barn by then.

Because the fire was spotted quickly, the Hartwoods and Elvers, who had been drinking outside the settling, had arrived in time to drag out bales that had caught and had smothered the flaming scraps on the floor. With the human chain bringing water, they were able to save the barn, and attention shifted to the blazing bales that might threaten the barn from outside.

Vern Hartwood rushed from the barn, shouting and waving something in the air. Firelight glinted on the brandished object, and people crowded around to inspect it before turning to search our line.

"For goodness' sake…" Kip gripped my arm. "Come on, Robin. Time we left."

Guided firmly out of the line and into the shadows, I turned as Eden entered the barn. After that, I had to concentrate on my footing as Kip pulled me unceremoniously from the field.

"Where are we going?"

"Back to the forge. Eden will bring your things later."

"Why? What's happened? What was Vern waving around?"

"A knife. A small knife with initials on the handle." Kip's head turned to me. "RH."

I tripped on a tussock, but Kip's grip held me firm, and we hardly paused as we reached the path.

"You mean my knife? The one that was stolen from school?"

"They found it in the barn, near where the fire started."

"Is that why we're running away?" My breath was catching now as we hurried along the track. "They can't believe I fired the barn. I've been at the party all evening."

"That has been pointed out, but you know what some of them are like, especially after a few drinks."

It didn't make sense. I must be missing something.

Into my head came a memory of the vigil at Ira's funeral pyre. I remembered sideways glances from groups of villagers and, later, Vern's hostility at school.

"Sorcery! Is that what they're claiming? Surely, they can't seriously–"

"Not when they stop and think about it, Robin. But, for some reason, the Hartwoods are stirring things up. Best not to wait around. Give them time to think it through."

I was shivering when we reached the forge. But Elm had already arrived with the tarlings and built the fire up before putting them to bed. We were warming beside it when Brook and Eden arrived with my purple cloak. Brook was quick to reassure us.

"It was Fin who left the knife behind. That's why Vern was keen to divert attention from the barn. The

Hartwoods had tried to hide other stuff Fin left behind, but their neighbours, the Elvers, recognised the things Eden brought out. They knew what had been taken, because the Hartwoods had made such a fuss about them when Fin disappeared.

"So, Fin set fire to the barn?"

Eden answered Kip.

"It looks like an accident. An oil lamp fell behind some bales that were screening a corner from the doorway. Behind the bales were remains of a blanket and other things from the house, so it was probably where Fin's been sleeping."

"Do you think Fin panicked and ran?"

"It must have seemed a better option than facing the Hartwoods." Eden's face was streaked with ash.

Brook was mulling cider to warm us. "I would have expected Fin to be away from Fendle by now."

Eden wasn't so sure.

"Sometimes the best place to hide is under everyone's nose. On home territory, you know which buildings aren't likely to be used for a while. You might even get a chance to sneak back home for something you'd forgotten while everyone's out looking for you. You'd know where food can be found. And when the hunt has died down, you can slip onto a cart out of the village. Better than walking for days in the cold."

Brook handed out the warm beakers. "You sound as if you speak from experience."

"Not mine, but I know many who have."

I sipped the spiced cider and its warmth spread outwards to meet that of the fire penetrating my chill.

"I should go home before I fall asleep."

"Do you have to?" asked Brook. "Why not stay here tonight?"

"I should get back to Fern. If anyone turned up to make trouble, she can't get away from the cottage."

"I'll go and get Fern," said Kip. "Who'll come with me to help herd the pups?"

Eden agreed. "We made sure word got around – about how the fire started and how your knife got there – but you're better off here tonight. I should go soothe the Fletchers. It's been an interesting evening."

Both stood, and Eden turned to me.

"I meant to give you Jay's knife earlier, but I forgot to mention it. I've left it on the mantelpiece in your cottage."

"Thank you." I looked up at Eden, whose face was expressionless again. "Thank you for all your help. We've kept you here too long."

Kip and Elm left with Eden to shepherd dogs along School Lane.

As I turned from the door, Brook's eye caught mine. "It's a shame the settling was interrupted. Taz has no excuse now; they'll be away to Tarfen soon."

I said, "I expect Morgan and Rowan will be pleased to have Eden home again."

Brook's brows rose.

"I'm sure Rowan will. Morgan died in a riding accident five summers ago. Didn't you know?"

Day Nineteen

Jay

My head hurt. My eyes wouldn't open. Well, they might if I tried harder, but I didn't want to risk it. I had drunk too much strong cider and barley wine. (*Storm tasted of barley wine.*)

My heart hurt. A hollow ache, as if my chest were bruised from inside. After I left the inn, Storm had nudged at my thoughts, but I closed my mind and drank more cider to dull the pain. Later in the night, I recalled Storm trying to rouse me, but I'd curled away with my elbows over my ears and felt sick.

Or it might have been a dream.

(*I'll never feel Storm close again.*)

My hand hurt. I must have abused it in my drunken state last night.

(*Storm isn't here to bind it.*)

The fallen leaves beneath me rustled if I moved. My stomach coiled. I remembered the last time I ate (*with Storm*).

I remembered my dinner's return after being woken. As if conjured by the memory, an odour reached me, and the sound of buzzing. I struggled to part my eyelids and peered through eyelashes at the flies circling a shining pool in the leaves close to my head. I rolled away, groaning, and my head throbbed as if something was about to burst out of it.

My throat tightened, sweat broke out on my forehead, and I closed my eyes again to shut out the light. A higher pitched humming zoomed past my ear – one of those airborne noises you can never locate till it bites you.

Above me, a bird sang a single note, over and over, with an upward lilt… "Chirp?"

Again, and again, and again, and again… "Chirp?"

"Chirp?" – *What now?*

"Chirp?" – *Where's your new life now?*

"Chirp?" – *How will you face your family now?*

How indeed? I couldn't go back. I'd proved them right; I wasn't to be trusted with the family business. Whether or not I returned, they would now have to complete the order without me.

Storm's thoughts nudged mine, still nearby. I opened one eye again, but quickly closed it against the pain and closed my mind as firmly. But the thoughts still surfaced.

How could I have been so gullible?

How could I be so irresponsible, chasing a daydream?

How could I, now, in the next minutes, make myself move, get up, function?

More to the point, how in hell's name would I find my way home through two counties with no guide, no money, one good hand, and not a single bloody survival skill to my name?

As consciousness returned, I was shivering with the cold

I struggled to my feet, trying not to jolt my injured hand. The splints were dislodged. I did my best to restore them, but the hand was throbbing again, like my head.

Every step was an effort. I stumbled from the trees and faced the Blasted Oak across the road. A familiar figure sat on the bench outside, gnawing on a leg of some fowl and watching the line of trees. I had wondered how I would face my family; I was about to find out. I stumbled to the bench and dropped beside Cris, jarring my pounding head.

"Don't let me interrupt your breakfast. What are you doing here?"

"It's lunch, actually. I came to find you; more precisely, to warn you. Ira's gone missing. Popular opinion has it you've disposed of the old battle-axe."

"Me?" Was this a joke? I was in no mood for jokes.

Cris wasn't smiling.

"Why me?"

"Your knife was on the floor of the cottage. With blood on it." Cris's expression was noncommittal.

"My knife?" I held my head in both hands, trying to calm the pounding while I struggled to make sense of this.

"I lost it. It wasn't in its sheath." Cris nodded and relaxed. "How did you know where to find me?"

"Mikki said you were camping by a lake and the innkeeper at the Green Man told me where the nearest one was…" words spilled now as if a dam had been breached, "…so I found your camp, but you weren't there. I rode around, looking, and then went back to wait for you. I gave up when it started getting dark. Thought I'd go back next day, but when I did, you'd packed up and gone."

Cris had been our stalker!

"I waited back at the fair for you to turn up. Danni was convinced you were planning to go to Scarth, but that didn't seem likely… not without telling someone. I realised then, pet, that something must have gone wrong. Samphire said they'd be taking this Storm home to Scarth with the Seagen convoy, so I helped with the packing up and came with them."

166

Cris's voice was rising and fading.

Everything ached. My stomach churned. The world swayed around me.

"When we came up the road Storm was sat here on this bench looking worried and when Sam said who I was, I thought the poor pet was going to cry with relief. If I hadn't turned up, I don't think your Storm would've–"

"Not *my* Storm!" I snarled, and then groaned as my head pounded harder. I felt sick again, but there was nothing left in my stomach. I started to my feet and discovered there was something left after all. A fitting conclusion to the whole bloody week, I thought – as far as I was able to formulate any coherent thought before I passed out.

When I woke again, I was back in the Blasted Oak, in the bed we'd argued on the previous night. My mouth tasted as if I'd died in my sleep and started to rot. I pushed away thoughts of Storm to find thoughts of Fendle waiting behind them. My lost knife had resurfaced just as Ira disappeared, and my absence will have fuelled suspicion. Assembly justice could be haphazard, and my family had no money or influence.

Since I was unable to help them anyway, would it be best if I stayed away?

Stings and scratches tormented me after my night in the undergrowth, but they faded in comparison to the throbbing of my hand. When Cris noticed I was awake, we changed the dressing, and the fingers looked hot and angry. Their wounds had opened again and were seeping; I must have damaged it while I was drunk.

Robin

I lay between sleeping and waking, knowing I was in a dream but unable to move.

The dream was of fire. I was alight but knew no pain, only the choking as I tried to breathe in smoke. At last I awoke, gasping, fully awake now and able to move.

I had been here before, halfway between a nightmare and the dark cottage silence broken only by Ira's snores. One recurring dream was of scuttling like rats through tunnels, while heavy thuds pounded above us. Another was of birds flying past as I dropped from a building higher than any building could be while it crumbled beneath me. My stomach's lurch would wake me from such dreams.

On this day, no snores broke the cottage silence, and I blessed the vixen outside when she screamed to assure me I was back in this world.

In the morning, Eden turned up at school for the key and hadn't returned it by lunchtime.

At the cottage, I found water boiling for tea, with fresh bread and cold meat set out for a meal. There was more than enough for two.

"You should have mentioned. I don't come home for lunch every day."

"In that case, I would have eaten my lunch before leaving. Camomile, mint or ginger?"

We sat at the table. Most of our conversations seemed to be conducted across one table or another. Eden was unusually buoyant, no doubt at the prospect of going home.

"Taz and I are leaving for Tarfen the day after tomorrow. If it's all right with you, I'll take Bracken tomorrow evening so that we can leave early next morning."

"You've decided on a name then? It's a nice name." I'd half expected "Pup".

"I stopped off at Cutler's Forge this morning on my way here. Brook's been telling me how much Kip enjoyed taking your class."

"Yes, I know. It was good of them; they need all hands to help with the order for the new inn."

"Oh. I see." Eden deflated.

I fell back on my usual practice of filling the silence.

"I think the 'lings would sooner be taught by Kip, to be honest. I've had so much time off it's taking me a while to get back into it. I'm not so desperate to get away from the house as I used to be."

Then I realised what I was saying and shut up. I looked up from my tea and across the table, but my confession had fallen on deaf ears. Eden had brightened a little but still didn't sound hopeful.

"So, I suppose you wouldn't be interested in a change of job?"

"That depends. What kind of job?"

"It would involve a move to Tarfen."

Ah! "Probably not," I admitted. "What did you have in mind?"

"It's just that I know one of the schools wants another teacher. They haven't started interviewing yet. It's only part time and wouldn't pay much, but it would fit nicely around something else I'm thinking of."

After pausing to view my reaction, the bid continued. So far, I wasn't tempted.

"It would be useful if we had someone we could consult about poisons and related matters, as cases arise. I could only pay you case by case, I'm afraid, when we need the help. Probably not worth thinking about. It was just an idea I was playing with."

"Do you get many poisonings?" Tarfen sounded altogether more dangerous than Fendle.

"We've had two in the last few weeks but, to be honest, I think they were both accidental."

That sounded more familiar. "People do often mistake poisonous plants for edible ones. Or it might be safe to eat certain parts of a plant, but not all of it."

"Exactly. People brought up in a town rarely know much about plants that grow on common land. We just see something that looks like free food. Everyone knows to be careful about mushrooms, but few of us know much else about what grows wild."

"It sounds as if some education for the adults wouldn't go amiss, never mind the schoolchildren."

"The thing is, I don't want to panic Tarfen about a serial poisoner, but I don't have the knowledge to say with confidence that these deaths were accidental. Maybe there is a mad poisoner around, but I don't know why anyone would bother. Both victims, if that's what they were, lived on their own, so I don't know if anything was taken from their rooms."

"Did they know each other?"

"If they did, they don't seem to have had other friends."

"Surely there's somebody in all of Tarfen you can ask about poisons?"

"I do ask, but the healers are busy spreading themselves thinly around people who aren't dead yet, and I can't keep bodies waiting around indefinitely for their burning. The payment I can offer isn't going to tempt anyone into letting me jump the queue. I'm not selling this job very well, am I?"

I half-smiled. "That's because you don't believe in it yourself. Actually, it sounds interesting, and I hope you find someone who can help. But my life's here, my friends are here. And I'm going to be late for work!"

I'd forgotten the time. I had been interested in the subject, if not the job. While talking about work, Eden had relaxed. Before any more was said, I sensed the return to formality. It was as if the air in the room had cooled.

"Of course. I'm sorry, I've rambled on… I'll clear up here and bring you the key."

"Thanks." I smiled my gratitude. "And, of course, take Bracken whenever you're ready."

Eden came with the key soon after class began but didn't linger to chat with the tarlings this time. It was a forlorn moment. The first of my pups had a name and a new owner. I did want good homes for them all… even so, I mourned her looming departure.

Day Twenty

Jay

I'd meant to leave a note and slip away early, but I slept for most of the day into the evening and still had to be shaken awake. Cris wanted to change my dressing.

The discharge oozing from my broken nails smelled of hung meat. We cleaned the mess and left it un-dressed overnight, but by morning it hadn't dried over and the stench lingered. Cris said we should leave in the morning for High Wenn and find a healer there.

The innkeeper nodded to Cris as we left. It was a nod that spoke volumes. Among other things, it told me that Cris had been told of my vociferous departure on the night of the argument. What, exactly, had Storm told them?

I watched the world we rode through from somewhere deep inside my head. I wasn't part of that world. Memories surfaced when my guard weakened, to add their pain to the throbbing arm and remind me how stupid I'd been.

Each memory opened my thoughts to Storm's seeking. I dare not contact Robin, for fear of letting Storm in, so I tried not to think of anything at all. I was happy for Cris to do the talking as we rode. I registered little of what was said, but in the chatter I read relief at being homeward bound.

"Kyl was busy with tearful farewells, so it made more sense for me to help with the packing up instead of chasing around the countryside looking for you when I wouldn't have known where to look anyway.

"Mikki's got your notes for Brook, about what's being delivered and when to expect it. Oh – and I sold the rest of Elm's knives to that big shop in High Wenn that seems to sell everything. Danni was telling them about yours, pet, and drew them a picture. They seemed interested. There might be an order in it if you take it to show them. When you have it back…" Cris faltered.

Would I get my knife back?

I doubted I'd be making another. Unless I could somehow use my frozen right hand for steadying…

No, it was too much to think about. "Where did they find the knife?"

"On the floor of Robin's cottage."

Robin…

"How is Robin taking it all?"

Cris stared at me, wondering. I must have looked as grim as I felt.

"Rob's been defending you to anyone who'll listen. Aren't you two…"

The rush of relief was unsteadying. I remembered I was a long way from the ground.

" 'Struth, Jay! You're white as a sheet! You sure you're alright? Now you've gone green."

We stopped to rest.

Gravity helps when you're getting off a horse, but it's still a challenge one-handed. Actually, one hand would have been easier. I could've used my right arm more confidently if my left hadn't kept wanting to get involved.

When safely seated, I sipped from the water flask.

"You think whoever took my knife broke into the cottage and attacked Ira?"

"Doesn't seem to matter what any of us think. Jess has decided you disposed of Ira and dropped the knife in the process."

"Careless of me." What had I done lately to annoy Jess? Other than evasive action.

Maybe that was enough. "So, you came to warn me. Should I expect a lynching on my return to Fendle, or a welcoming party?"

That wasn't fair of me. Rob must be frantic. "Robin must be worried about Ira."

"Robin's worried about you too, pet. An investigator's coming from Tarfen – an Administrator, no less! Assembly Guards might be meeting the convoy as we speak, to take you off before Fendle."

"Really? They're taking it that seriously?"

"It's called protective supervision, apparently. We thought you should be prepared."

I remembered something else. "Should you be riding around the countryside right now, with the baby due and everything?

"Don't be ridiculous. There's weeks to go yet."

None of this seemed real.

But Cris had come all this way to warn me, so it must be real.

I couldn't worry about it now. In a minute, I would have to begin the clumsy process of getting, one-handed, back on my feet. Just the thought of standing made me dizzy.

Robin

The convoy's back.

Jay isn't with them. Neither is Cris.

Brook came into school at the end of the day to tell me. Danni had been amusing the workshop with tales of a mysterious stranger called Storm from an unknown land beyond Seacrag, who Jay had gone off with. The Seagen expected Storm to meet up with them on their way home, so Cris had gone with them to find Jay.

Brook invited me back to the forge, and I promised to come along later. My stomach rebelled at the mention of food, but the Cutlers would be worried about Cris and glad of someone to talk it out with. There's often reassurance in sharing a worry. And I might learn more about this Storm person.

I stopped at the cottage to feed Fern and the pups and watched them eat, to make sure the littlest one didn't get pushed out – the one Kip had chosen.

I found Mikki with the horses and asked how Cris had been when they parted. It seemed a natural concern for a foster-sib. Mikki gave instead a colourful opinion of Jay's stupidity, and I wondered why I had come, or what I had hoped to hear. When I said it sounded a romantic tale the way Danni told it, Mikki calmed down and looked at me with sympathy, which was worse than the anger.

"Robbie, I know Jay wouldn't hurt you for the world, but… perhaps it's as well they left when they did."

Jay had spoken about me then. My face burned as hot as Mikki's looked.

"Yes. I'm sure Jay means well." I summoned my most convincing smile. "Thanks, Mikki. I must go. Kip and Brook are expecting me."

This seemed to reassure Mikki, who patted my shoulder and said I would be okay.

At the forge I heard the tale again from Elm and there was nothing more I could ask. We ate together, but I wasn't hungry – just empty. The tarlings were subdued, but livened up as Cris took them off for bed.

Brook pressed me to stay longer, and they tried to draw me into conversation. I was too distracted, and they gave up the attempt, but the sound of their voices was a soothing backdrop to my thoughts.

I had looked forward to Jay's return with trepidation, fearing proximity might undermine my good intentions. But no return at all was somehow worse. If I felt this way now, would my resolve have held if Jay came home?

The years to come would be different without Jay. Kip, Brook, and Mikki weren't the only ones who'd assumed we would settle together. Half of Fendle would be pitying me.

The other half would avoid me in case I put a hex on them.

My future stretched ahead… school on six days of the week, staying home on the seventh, and going to school again on the next six. Occasionally, Brook and Kip would invite me to supper, and so would Elm and Cris. I might take up whittling, or painting, or brewing potions. In time, news would arrive of Jay's new life and new family. They might even come and visit.

No. I wouldn't do this!

"Are you all right, Robin?" I must have been quiet for too long. "You look pale. Would you like me to take the class for you tomorrow?"

"Say yes," Brook suggested, trying to keep things light, but looking concerned. "Any excuse would do."

"You really do enjoy it, don't you?" I asked, to be sure.

Kip's eyes met mine. "I really do."

Nobody spoke while I digested this. There was an air of expecting more.

"It's just… there's a job going in Tarfen. But it doesn't sound much of an offer." I kept my eyes on my hands and the cup between them.

"This is from Eden?"

"Partly."

I glanced up, but they were looking at each other, not me.

"What kind of job, Robin?'

I told them of the school vacancy and Eden's idea and the part-time nature of the whole proposition. I didn't make it sound viable at all. I didn't mention the ideas I'd had myself about what else I might do there.

"But I can't just walk out on the school, and anyway you're needed here, Kip."

Then Brook said, "I think it sounds interesting."

Kip agreed. "And I'd be getting paid for the teaching. Right now, we could use the money. I've never apprenticed as a smith. In normal circumstances, I mostly keep track of the bookkeeping and chase up the bills and tinker with new designs. I can do that in the evenings or Funday."

"But if Jay isn't here, you'll be needed in the forge as well."

Brook dismissed this. "There are always likely apprentices leaving school. Cris and I can take turns on the fairs. More to the point, is it what you want to do?"

I didn't know.

"It doesn't sound much of a proposition. Half the income is hypothetical. It would depend on what turns up. And I'd be leaving everyone... I'd miss you all."

I knew nobody in Tarfen. It was a daft idea altogether.

"It's worth considering, Robin. You know we'll miss you, too."

That was a prediction, not a persuasion. It panicked me.

"I'm not convinced. I'll go home and sleep on it."

But that wasn't what I did at all. I tossed and twisted all night.

Day Twenty-one, Robin

I wasn't surprised to see Kip on my doorstep next morning, long before I was ready to leave for work.

Not that I was *un*ready. I was washed, dressed, fed – sort of – the table was clear, and I sat gazing at the opposite wall, registering nothing. My body was ready; my mind was a mess. The door creaked, and when I turned, Kip was peering around it.

"All right if I come in?"

"Of course you can."

"I've come to check if you still want to go in, or would you like me to take them this morning?"

"That's kind of you," I began, before registering a hopeful note along with the concern in the question. "You'd like to, wouldn't you?"

"I'm bored at home while we're waiting for the metal to arrive. I've got used to doing more with my time. Since I've been filling in for you, everyone's reorganised my work between them." Kip grinned. "It's humbling to find one is not, after all, indispensable."

"That's because you've trained them all so well." A thought occurred to me. "I suppose if you're good at training people up, you'll eventually do yourself out of a job."

"The aim of every parent," said Kip.

"Come in with me anyway," I said. "The class will be pleased to see you, and we can do something more interesting with them if there are two of us. And we need to work out what I owe you for the past couple of weeks; yesterday was payday. You've earned more of it than I have."

"For goodness' sake… don't be ridiculous. You'll need it if you decide to go to Tarfen."

"You need it now."

Kip shrugged dismissively in the way of Jay. How alike they were in many respects. Cris was more Brook.

I was prepared for an argument. I had only one of me to feed now, unless you counted Fern. A trapped rabbit or a fish lasted us a couple of days, and I still had roots to harvest from the garden. At Cutler's Forge, they were cutting corners and had no money coming in until the inn's order was paid for.

"We can talk about it later." Kip settled in the chair opposite me, prepared to stay until I answered properly. "Have you thought any more about the job in Tarfen?"

I'd thought of little else. "Would you like some tea?"

"You know you can always come back to us if things don't work out." With my tail between my legs… nothing new about that. "Especially if it's me holding the job for you."

"You sound as if you're trying to get rid of me."

"Robin, if Jay comes back…"

I'd been here before, wondering if Jay would come back this time. Each time, I'd slipped back so easily into our well-trodden path. I probably would again.

If Jay came back.

How weak that sounded, even in my own thoughts? "If Jay comes home, with or without this Storm, it won't change a thing for me now."

And if not, what was here for me but memories?

"And if not, don't underestimate the value of having the four – six – seven of you practically next door."

"Tarfen isn't so far – less than a day's travel. You'd make new friends there. Eden will have friends too, and family. You'd meet people at the school… start again."

I knew everyone in Fendle. (Most were settled by my age, with 'lings of their own.) Tarfen was big and busy and unknown. Nobody knew me there. (Nobody had known Ira.)

Was I strong enough to build a new life?

A life without two of my disabilities – Ira and Jay. The kink I could cope with.

Kip's opinion was clear. "We'd be here if you need us. There's always a room for you at Cutler's Forge."

Voices passed by on the path.

"Oh bugs! I must go. They'll be waiting outside to be let in." Kip conceded defeat and rose to leave. "Come in with me, Kip. They'll forgive me then for making them wait outside."

Standing, Kip nearly trod on a puppy. "That reminds me, can I take this little one home with me today? We're going to call her Pickle."

"That's a good name. How do you think she'll get on with Marmalade?"

"I think he'll mistake her for a rat and eat her," Kip replied placidly.

Halfway through the morning, I gave up any pretence that I was contributing to the lesson, and I went home to think.

I told Kip I was going to say goodbye to Pickle, and to come and collect her at lunchtime.

When Kip arrived, I was sitting in the same chair as before, with little Pickle on my lap, gently chewing at my fingers. I heard the door open and close, and Kip came again to sit facing me.

"I'm going to do it, Kip. I'm going to Tarfen."

Now I had said it; I had committed myself.

Immediately, I changed my mind.

But, despite my misgivings, a germ of excitement was sprouting. Was I being weak – running away? Should I stay and face down the gossips?

Kip was practical as ever.

"You must go now and tell Eden. They're planning to leave tomorrow."

Day Twenty-three

Jay

I surfaced unwillingly, leaving behind both Storm and Robin in my dream.

For the past day, I'd been drifting in and out of consciousness. At High Wenn, a healer said three fingers must come off now, if I wasn't to lose more than fingers.

The knife cut quick and clean, but the potion used to numb the pain left me barely conscious. Now, as I awoke, I tried to return to my dream, but the images blurred and faded, the way dreams do.

I hadn't the will to guard my thoughts. They must have seemed deranged, but Storm's answering concern had flowed through my senses like balm; heartfelt and unmistakeable. Robin's presence, when it came, was comforting, but brief, with attention directed elsewhere. I had neglected Rob too long. The distance between us was more than just cart tracks.

My waking self reassured me that the journey would bring us closer, although my first plan had been to slip away from Cris and High Wenn to consider my future – an unrealistic goal, like most of my goals. Groggy as I was, though, I insisted I was well enough to travel. I wouldn't be much use at home, but they needed Cris.

Now we had spent more of the fair's earnings on a healer and beds for the night. I had much to make up for, and no idea how.

I hadn't expected my ghost fingers to still hurt, but the rest of the hand was firmly bound and padded against accidental knocks. They told us it shouldn't need re-dressing until we reached home, unless it got wet, or the smell returned.

If we held our pace, we'd be home tomorrow. I slipped into a doze, jerking awake barely in time to stop myself sliding off Swift. To keep myself awake, I talked. Cris must have wondered at my transformation from deaf-mute to chatterbox.

"You should be home by now. That potion was too strong. I took too long to recover."

"Mustn't grumble. The healers know what they're doing."

I grunted. Minutes later, I was drifting again.

I sat straighter. "What are you planning to call the new tarling?"

"We thought, Ember."

"A fitting name for a smith." I nodded. "You'll have used up the best names before I start breeding," although neither of us expected that to be any time in the foreseeable future. Perhaps it was time for me to grow up and settle down. "Remind me again when Ember's due?"

"Not till spring: a winter away."

I remembered the months after the births of the others – infant wails in the darkness, and night-time shufflings.

"Babies seem to be hard work."

Cris turned with a smile. "Trust me, they're worth it."

Don't trust anyone who says, "Trust me". I remembered the sentiment, if not the context, and Storm was no longer dormant but in the forefront of my thoughts. We'd spent more nights apart now than we'd spent together.

But I couldn't talk to Cris about Storm. Unhappiness doesn't work like cake. It isn't halved when you share it. I searched instead for Robin, and Storm withdrew.

Rob wasn't to be summoned. I gave up and tried to think of nothing at all. Ira's disappearance and my lost knife formed a cloud that wouldn't go away and grew darker as we neared Fendle. I couldn't do anything about it now. But my usual strategy for putting thoughts aside wasn't working. I'd too many things to put out of my mind and little else to replace them with.

Memories nudged at each other, blurring and merging as Swift's gentle jog set me drifting again. One memory surfaced from the jumble, of riding beside Storm as we sang to rouse the forest. A stab of loss pierced my lethargy, and I was back on the road to Fendle riding beside tone-deaf Cris. I wanted to howl like a dog, but I hadn't the energy.

We stopped by a river to eat. As fish wove through reeds, I pulled a thread from my overshirt to tie around a scrap of dry meat and lay with my bait suspended from the bandaged hand hovering just above the water. The fish ignored it. My arm soon ached, and the hand throbbed, so I dropped the thread with its meat. The thrashing as fish converged on it drew Cris's attention.

"Feeding the fish? Shame we don't have a line. One of those would make a good supper."

"Storm caught ours without a line or a net." My voice sounded distant in my own ears.

"How? Can you do it?" I hauled myself to my feet in an ungainly, one-handed fashion and turned my back on the river in disgust.

"Apparently not."

Cris gathered our things and started packing them away. "Probably just as well, pet. You couldn't hold it without getting your bandage wet."

Which I should have thought of myself.

The horses were fresh from their rest, but I still had to concentrate to stay upright. I steeled myself to stay awake.

"One finger and a thumb won't grip metal firm for striking, either. Or hold silver steady for fine etching. I won't be much use in the forge, and it's been demonstrated that I'm not a great deal of use at anything else."

Cris protested. "Who says that?"

"Events have demonstrated it." I was surprised to hear myself sounding drunk. "I've demonstrated it. There's bog-all I can do to support myself, other than going on the streets." *Storm knew what I was good at.* "I'm useless at anything that matters."

Cris frowned. "Stop feeling sorry for yourself. You're good at lots of things. Selling for a start. You had those apprentices running the stall as if they'd been doing it for years. Wasn't it their first trip?"

I kept my eyes on the road and didn't answer. Cris carried on anyway.

"I spotted our stall straight away when I got there. It stood out from the other side of the field."

"That's just a cheap trick to catch the eye… shouting with colours."

"Well, nobody else did it. They were shouting in words, and you couldn't tell one cry from another. The youngsters changed the display twice in a day, so that people who came past would look again. I don't imagine they thought of that on their own. Mikki says the stall was up and selling in half the time the other pitches took."

Because I'd wanted to get away with Storm.

"They knew what to do when you weren't there, and they'll know what to do next time."

"There you are then; they can do it without me. I am no longer required. That's hardly a way I can earn a living, is it? Making myself redundant? It's not a skill to earn me a bed for the night or food in my belly."

Cris had no answer to that because I was right.

The clouds thickened through the afternoon, angry grey billows rolling over empty grey fields. We travelled on familiar home ground now, but that didn't make it any less bleak and unwelcoming.

As we made camp, a swarm of starlings flew over in a single twittering cloud. Robin always stops to watch the starlings. These touched down in a field and rose again like one giant bird.

I hadn't really appreciated the wide openness of Tarn before. It was just home, after all. In Wendale, trees and hedgerows screened neighbouring fields from the track.

That night Storm finally left me but, home or not, I still couldn't find Robin.

Robin

Everything had happened so quickly my head was still reeling.

Kip took charge of the pups and was supervising the rehomings. My things had been sent on with Taz's the previous day. My last-minute change of mind had delayed the Administrators' return, but Taz was happy to have another day in Fendle. I had been prepared to follow later – Brook offered to take me – but we were overruled.

On the day we left, I was ready early with Fern and Bracken, but my courage hadn't time to waver before Eden came for us. When we collected Taz, any sadness the Fletchers felt at the departure was successfully concealed. I may have detected an echo of popping cork as we descended the grand front steps, just before the door closed. The family all waved from a front window as our wagon drove away.

I would be found a room in the Assembly buildings; Eden didn't seem to see this as a problem. Tonight, Fern, Bracken and I would stay at the Blue Shiel Inn, while Eden went on to the Thatchers, who lived just outside Tarfen, to see Rowan. Eden and Rowan would return to their Assembly apartment in the morning. Bracken was to be a surprise and would stay with me until they were home in Tarfen.

All this was explained on the journey. It was touching to see Eden's excitement in anticipation of seeing Rowan again, especially from someone who was normally so reserved. Taz was subdued. Might Fendle soon have a vacancy to fill in the Assembly of Administrators?

I doubt I would have taken it all in if Eden hadn't relayed it so often. I was still dazed. I had told myself I could do this until the phrase became meaningless, and I began to wonder again if I really wanted to. Eden's repetitions did nothing to familiarise the juxtaposition of "home" and "Tarfen", words which weren't linked in my world. I had just left my home. I had mislaid budding hopes of a new beginning somewhere in the chaos of the past day. Already I was missing Brook and Kip, and even my class.

The skies above Tarn were overcast as our cart trundled past the desolate winter fields.

Just outside Tarfen, I spotted a dead bird on the track, partly eaten and discarded by some animal. Carts had ridden over it, flattening it into the dust. It looked like a crow until we drove past, and I saw the dirty white matted feathers under the black. I told myself a dead magpie didn't count and touched my silver teardrop earring for luck.

Day Twenty-four, Jay

On the last night of our journey, I had settled myself for sleep when Storm found me. Our thoughts met, and I hadn't the energy to block the incoming regret.

Having registered I was still alive, if unresponsive, Storm then left me alone. I knew an aching emptiness where Rob should be. Surely, I could find Robin this close to Fendle if I searched hard enough and long enough. My body knew better.

But when I woke, Robin still didn't answer to my searching. It was lonely in my head on my own.

I fought to stay upright in the saddle though fields and sky shimmered around me. I'd already caused Cris enough delay. The horses sensed home nearby and hardly needed direction.

We took a brief break. I crumbled my bread while watching a sparrowhawk hang motionless above a nearby watercourse. It dived without warning, and something struggled in its grip as it climbed again, heading towards Fendle. I wished we could follow that way, across the fields, but we must trek around them.

Home was a hearthlight beckoning from the end of a misty tunnel. Tomorrow I would curl up and lick my wounds while Robin soothed my weeping insect bites with salve.

The wind strengthened. Back on horseback, its gusts nearly blew me off again. Clouds whipped overhead, lashing us with needles of rain on their way. I dismissed Cris's concern; we couldn't stop now. Robin was a warm, comforting thought to cling to, like a tarling's favourite blanket.

By the time we reached Fendle, it was the barn owl that hunted the dykes. Fendle slumbered, its villagers at home with their families.

My brain had stopped communicating with my hands and feet, so Cris settled the horses alone while I sat on a straw bale and shivered. Elm sensed Cris's return and came to find us. Between them, they kept me upright and hoisted me into the house.

The hot food and mulled cider on offer would have fed a litter of Cutlers. It was a shame I couldn't manage any of it. Around me they spoke of Ira. Cris's relief was tangible, but I barely registered why.

Robin could tell me about it tomorrow.

Tomorrow brought no enlightenment, nor the days after. For ten days I registered nothing as I lay in a fever. When it left me, I resurfaced with no energy or will to rouse myself. The news relayed at my bedside offered little incentive to rejoin the living.

Kip was Fendle's new teacher. Ira, my old adversary, was dead, and Robin was gone.

PART THREE: Leaving Fendle

Tarfen

Robin

The Assembly was housed in a former manor house, built mainly of stone around an open square. Before the Great Sickness, it had housed the Chief's family, but disease has no respect for rank, and this one had taken the family.

Two pairs of gates faced each other from opposite sides of the courtyard. Neither had been closed since reopening after the Sickness, and now nobody dared try in case they fell and crushed someone.

Offices and courts of the Upper and Lower Assemblies occupied adjoining sides of the building. Over the years, additions had been built on, extending into the courtyard or out to Tarfen's streets. Eden's office was tucked away in a far corner of the upper floor of the Administrators' wing.

The other two sides of the square housed rooms let to Administrators and Assembly workers at preferential rates. Ground-floor apartments boasted a patch of garden fenced off from the square. These were unpopular when Eden first arrived, upper apartments being easier to secure against the frequent break-ins. Now the Watchguards and Assembly guards shared responsibility for regular patrols of the area, and many who had called so loudly to be elevated now called equally loudly to return to their gardens.

The two rooms I had been assigned were up a rickety staircase tucked between two rush fences, one of which proved to be Eden's.

We met Rowan and Puss on the day I moved in. The carter delivered my boxes in the morning and helped us move them up to my rooms. As Eden and I unpacked my kitchen things, Fern and Bracken inspected the floors, paying particular attention to a gap in the corner by the fireplace. When I dropped Fern's blanket on the floor, she immediately claimed it, circling to nest it to her liking.

Rowan must have come home while we were moving furniture. Unsuspecting, we took the dogs downstairs and opened the gate to Eden's garden. The door to the apartment stood ajar, and Puss sat on the doorstep.

Seeing the dogs, she didn't wait to be introduced but shot across the patch of grass, followed by an excited Bracken as Fern barked encouragement. Rowan appeared at the door to see Puss leap into a chestnut tree overhanging the fence. The cat swished her tail at the puppy yapping below. Our attempts to coax her down only prompted Puss to move to a higher branch. In the excitement, Rowan didn't appear to notice that my shape was different.

As I'd imagined, the tarling was tall for nine summers but darker than Eden with hair of deep mahogany, which must have been Morgan's legacy. Rowan's sparkling eyes and ready child-white grin weren't very Eden-like either and, despite an unfortunate beginning, Bracken was making a friend.

Puss was less easily won over. She still hadn't descended when we finished lunch and Rowan had to return to school. Eden promised to climb and retrieve the cat if she didn't come down by herself. Although sceptical, Rowan left for school.

We took the dogs inside, where Eden made tea and told me more about Tarfen. Another cup later, Puss still hadn't moved. Was she stuck?

Eden made more tea; I learned about the Watchers and their work. Puss watched from her branch.

"It looks as if I'm going up the tree," Eden concluded with no enthusiasm.

With the dogs shut in the rooms, we went to survey the tree's trunk. This stood outside the garden, close to the fence. It was a solid old tree.

I reviewed the likely routes to reach Puss. "It doesn't look a bad climb."

The trunk conveniently split low down, with plenty of sturdy branches on the way up. Leaves had thinned so vision was relatively unimpeded, and it hadn't rained lately to make the boughs slippery. Puss watched us, unmoved.

Eden appeared in no hurry to get started, no doubt anticipating every hand-hold with that forethought I'd learned to expect from this meticulous planner.

"Yes. Right. Here we go then."

A scramble and a heave later, and Eden wobbled with knees bent, one hand on the trunk and the other clinging to the branch above. Puss looked unimpressed.

"Are you all right up there?" I asked.

"I will be when I've got my bearings. I'm … um … not good at heights."

In a moment of silence as Eden's legs slowly straightened, all became clear.

"That's why you didn't go into the family business."

"It contributed to my decision," Eden agreed tightly.

I made a decision of my own. "Come on down. You can catch me if I fall."

"You can't climb up here!" Vehemence caused Eden to wobble again.

"Just watch me!"

I started up the other side of the tree without waiting for Eden to descend. I wasn't serious anyway, about being caught if I fell. I may be short, but I have heavy bones. Eden's looked so slender, I might break them.

"I trained on the spindly growths of Fendle. This is a stepladder in comparison."

Our tree-climbing summers hadn't been wasted. Jay would have been proud of me. Ira would have had a fit. The cat watched with interest.

The boughs further up looked less substantial; would they take my weight?

I edged towards Puss, who looked less complacent as the branch shook. I paused and spoke to her in what I meant to be a reassuring manner, hoping she didn't run further up the tree.

Was that a creak?

A crack? I backed to the trunk.

Puss sprang down in three leisurely leaps, away from the tree, over the fence and into the garden. She launched herself through the open window to the sound of frenzied yapping and an encouraging bark from Fern.

Eden's indecision was visible – whether to rush and rescue the cat or stay to catch me if I fell.

I descended covered with bits of twig and damp bark before a decision was reached. As we skirted the fence, the barking stopped. Our eyes met in dismay and we ran, half expecting to find the dogs making an early meal on the other side of the door.

I was relieved to find Puss seated imperiously on a tall drawer chest, tail switching from side to side. Below her, Bracken's wagged in invitation. The pup glanced our way on entry, tongue waving at us from between her grinning teeth. Fern had settled on a comfy chair.

Eden found barley wine, and we sat with it on a stone bench in the garden until Rowan came home. Satisfied that Bracken hadn't harmed Puss, Ro made a fuss of both and decided that Bracken should stay in her new home to establish whether the two could survive a night together. When the time came, Fern left the last of her pups without a backward glance.

Next morning Ro found Bracken sleeping in the basket with Puss and ran up to share the news with me.

My rooms were airy, and the furniture worn but comfortable. Eden said former tenants had left it behind, but it seemed too good to have been abandoned. I threw colourful blankets over the chairs, and they felt like mine.

Fern spent her mornings with Bracken, and when I finished at school, I would go home to let them out.

Eden's garden was a blank page waiting to be filled. Although the grass was kept trimmed, nothing else grew there. The grasses in one corner were different though, lush and blue. They would soon die back as winter progressed, so I cut them to boil for dye, unsure what to expect. They reduced, eventually, to a rich, darkish teal.

The teachers at the school welcomed my arrival, having expected a longer campaign for more staff. On Oneday and Threeday mornings, I worked with one of them in their class. On Twodays and Fourdays, I took the morning class on a rota, while their teacher chased up those families whose tarlings hadn't been seen at school for a while. On

Fivedays, I took an older class whose teacher was out with a group, visiting a workshop.

Fiveday's visits often led to a pupil spending a week with a prospective employer, to prove their worth. Tarfen youngsters had more options than in Fendle, and more work opportunities existed for a third or fourth sibling. The head-teacher told me it had been Eden who'd initiated the workshop visits, keen to reduce the number of jobless school-leavers roaming the streets.

In Tarfen, no formal lessons were scheduled on Weeksend, so that children could instead learn more of their family's business. Although it was more likely they were allocated family chores or looked after small children while their parents did other things. On those days, the teachers cleaned classrooms and generally prepared for the following week. Since I had no classroom, they did not pay me to clean one, and Weeksend was a free day to spend as I chose.

After my morning school sessions, Eden sometimes joined Ro and me for lunch. Afterwards, we would walk back to school with Rowan and on to the Watchguards' office, which was where I came to spend most of my afternoons and Weeksends, and even the occasional Funday if my services were needed. There, I met Eden's assistants, Ash and Logan, a pair of pussycats, and Senior Administrator Jordan, who was more leonine.

This was the Administrator spoken of in Fendle as "our" Minstrer. Eden introduced me as Fendle's expert on poisons, a shameful exaggeration from one usually so precise.

"And this, Robin, is Senior Administrator Jordan Tarson, to whom our department owes its existence."

"Not quite, Ede. It took more than my word to convince the Upper Assembly."

It was a token protest. Jordan preened, as proud as a swan presenting its cygnet. And as watchful.

The Minstrer was not tall but exuded the authority of several years on the lower Assembly. Even so, this was one of the younger members – not much older than Mikki, I judged. With smooth, well-practised charm, Jordan asked if I would be staying long in Tarfen.

"I live here now. I'm teaching in Fallowfields School."

Eden felt it necessary to explain my presence. "When we have unexplained deaths, Robin's expertise will be invaluable."

"Really?" Eyes widened under unnaturally arched brows. I felt as useful as a woodlouse.

This dislike of me didn't fade with further acquaintance. Whenever we met, Jordan greeted me with the coolest formality, becoming positively icy as time passed. Eden's early reserve had been genial in comparison. I merely smiled and offered tea.

Whatever doubts Jordan may have harboured, Logan and Ash didn't share them. Both were keen to learn about poisons. I promised to teach them, but instruction was haphazard, since it was rare for us all to be in the office together. When they were called away, I usually stayed to keep the office open and take messages. Although unofficial, I spent most afternoons there and soon learned more about Tarfen's underside. The name of Giltin often came up, and one evening I queried this with Eden.

"For shiel's sake, don't mention it to *anyone*. I can't be seen to be investigating fellow Administrators until I have solid proof. And I don't want the Giltins covering their tracks before I have evidence."

"Of course not! What've they been up to?"

"I'm not sure yet how far Lex and Geri Giltin are involved, but Lex at least must have some idea what Jess is up to. I stayed with the Fletchers while I was in Fendle, and you know how ready Taz is to chat. It appears that over the years Jess has offered to take on more of the tax collection work and Taz has been happy to delegate it."

I said I thought Taz would be happy to quit altogether if it weren't for family pride. "The Fletchers bask shamelessly in the reflected glory of having a Minstrer in the family."

Eden's nose wrinkled. "Well, resignation might be the best option for Taz if irregularities come to light. There's sure to be comeback around neglect of duties. I made discreet enquiries about the local taxes while I was in Fendle. Everyone complains about paying too much tax, but it's true that those who didn't mind me knowing seem to be paying more than I'd expect from a village of Fendle's size and trades. Yet, when you look into Tarfen's treasury records, Fendle appears as a smaller and poorer village than it actually is."

"Jess is cheating both ends, then."

"Indeed. I suspect there's a clerk in the treasury getting paid to turn a blind eye, if not someone further up the tree."

"What will you do?"

"When I have enough evidence, I ought to clear it with an Advisor before I seize an Administrator. But since I don't know who else is involved, I might risk getting Jess safely locked up first. Fendle may find it needs to appoint new Administrators before winter's end.

"Unless it all goes horribly wrong, in which case it'll be the Watchguards in need of a new Administrator."

Fendle

Jay

When I returned to the shores of consciousness and found myself in my own bed, the throbbing had reduced to a dull ache and my remaining fingers didn't hurt so much.

They didn't move much either. Thumb and forefinger met as they should, but the claw had no power to clasp metal firmly for striking. I'd be little use in the forge, other than sweeping up.

Kip returned my knife to me, polished to a shine. I declined the rings from my right hand that Cris had held since High Wenn for safekeeping.

"Keep them for yourself, or Elm."

"Our fingers are wider, petal. They wouldn't fit."

"Give them to Kip then."

When Brook asked to borrow a pair of earrings one evening, I opened my display box to find someone had cleaned all those too. Their bright shining prompted me to remove my single tarnished hoop and restore equilibrium, at least to my ears. I was pleased to find my claw adequate to the task.

Clothes were another matter. I wore whatever was easiest to fasten, often the same as the day before, until Brook suggested I needed to change. The time I once spent deciding what to wear was greatly reduced. I had little else to do with the time thus saved, but I filled it as best I could.

Once strong enough to leave my bed, I helped in the kitchen, to strengthen my claw and learn what it was capable of. I spilled a lot. Belatedly, I learned the skills other tarlings picked up in childhood. Instead of learning to cook, I'd been carving beads out of acorns.

I took up carving again to see if my claw could hold the wood steady. I didn't dare try it with silver yet. Even so, I carved my fingers as often as the wood, which reminded me of the days when we practiced by carving wooden animals for the younger cousins. If Ira found our creations lying around, they'd end up as firewood, which roused Robin to fury. If spells could be cast by glares alone, Ira would've vanished in a puff of steam.

How was Rob faring in Tarfen?

Kip wondered too; I heard them talking in the next room. Brook thought that Eden was taken with Robin, but Brook wasn't good at reading people. Kip had dismissed the idea as fanciful.

I sank back into Cutler's Forge like a feather bed after a hard day. Some mornings I'd wake thinking I need only walk to the cottage and Rob would be there to listen. Then reality would surge in, like the river in a rainstorm, to wash away the dream and remind me Robin was gone. Now I was home, memories of Storm were mixed up with the journey and the fever. None of it seemed real.

Robin was real. Nobody understood my feelings like Robin; that must mean something.

On days like these, I had to get away. I took myself to the river, and the scruffy stray came too. I'd seen him trotting back from School Lane and thought his tail less jaunty than before, but by the river he became himself again. He'd follow his nose till I lost sight of him in the long grass, and suddenly spring into sight to pounce on a water vole. I never saw him catch anything.

Neither did I, till I gave up Storm's method of fishing in favour of hooks, with a net for landing. While I waited for the fish to forget about me, my thoughts wandered to places I'd once wanted to visit, their charm now tarnished.

So, what *did* I want now?

I had to repair this rift with Robin, before I could get on with the rest of my life. After that, I wanted the same things everyone else wanted – security, a warm hearth, and a full stomach.

The fish would bring me back to earth by stealing my bait. I'd feel the tug and see the biggest fish of the day swim away with a flick of its tail and my bait in its mouth. When the wind sent ripples across the river, it conjured up Sam's tales of the sea, and my thoughts drifted again. Sam said sailing was like flying on water.

Maybe my feet were best kept on the ground; they'd left it once too often.

My first catch was a modest one, but still brought a rare moment of pride. It motivated me to concentrate until I could provide an occasional evening meal to vary the fare of trapped rabbits or Sandy's donated hens. I even knew how long to cook it.

Now, when Sandy took out a hunting party, I joined them. I would never be an archer, but I could still throw a knife or set a trap. I practised with a slingshot on the tree-rats. Not the squirrels – it seemed unfair to take advantage of their tameness, although I expected I could overcome my misgivings if ever my supper depended on it. They watched my antics with curiosity in their dark, oval eyes, and their bushy red tails twitched when the dog barked at them. There was nothing so endearing about a mud-grey tree-rat with its beady black eyes and wormlike tail… until it was skinned and gutted and simmering in a pot.

With midwinter a few weeks away, the forge had completed little more than half of the hotel order. The only consolation was that building wasn't going well either. The inn wouldn't be ready for the grand midwinter festival they'd planned for an opening. Even so, we'd have to extend the loan… at an increased rate of interest.

Every day after school, Kip worked for a couple of hours in the forge. When I was allowed back, my contribution ran to tending fires and burnishing finished items, something the tarlings could've done equally well. I was less use than an apprentice.

One evening, I suggested we might borrow Danni from the Wysmiths, but Kip had already thought of that.

"They have their own order to fit out the stables. They've promised to send Danni over when it's finished."

Brook fretted. "I shouldn't have borrowed the money. We should have let the order go to Tarfen."

"You can't have known you'd be three workers short, with Cris away rescuing me, and Kip filling in for Robin…" I reminded myself it wasn't Brook I was angry with and released my grip on the goblet that was etching a groove in my palm. "And now I can't work anyway, and Kip's stuck at the school because Rob had enough of my–"

"Hold on! You can't take all the credit for that. I'm teaching because I want to, and Robin didn't leave on your account. The Tarfen job offer came up. And some of the villagers were getting nasty."

"Nasty how?" I'd thought most of them liked Rob, even sympathised, what with Ira and everything. What else had I failed to notice?

Brook frowned. "Only the usual troublemakers. They stirred themselves up when Ira disappeared and then they had no one to hound for it. Without Ira to vent their fears on, they need a new scapegoat to blame for everything."

I wasn't so sure. If I'd come home when I should, Rob would have been here, and we'd have sorted things out and faced them together. And if Kip and I had been working, the order would be nearing completion by now. Instead, they were struggling, with no stock left to sell, and no time to make any until this cursed order was completed. Everything Kip earned went on essentials like charcoal. We ate what we hunted or harvested from the garden – mostly Robin's garden, since none of us had fertile fingers.

"How about the cottage? It's yours now, isn't it, Kip – now you're running the school? Can't you let it out?" The Barley Mow was often fully booked. "Sandy could rent it as extra lodgings."

Kip stopped me before I started spending the proceeds. "It belongs to the school. I have the use of it if I need somewhere to live, but Jess and Taz would have something to say if we tried to rent it out. I expect it'll be offered to the next apprentice teacher when Ty moves on."

The thought of someone else living there was unsettling. I'd thought of us looking after it till its rightful tenant returned.

That evening Kip initiated me into the mysteries of bookkeeping. It was easy enough to follow, but I didn't see it as my life's work.

Still, beggars can't choose their scraps.

But if I didn't want to live off my parents, neither could I live off Robin. I needed an occupation that would justify my existence.

Midwinter

Robin

Rowan stayed with me now whenever Eden was called away for a day or two. This meant that Ro missed school less often, but it also meant Eden's parents saw less of their grandchild.

We visited the Thatchers for the midwinter celebrations to herald the birth of the new year. Jarith Thatcher was all Tarn, sparrow-brown, unassuming and reserved, like Eden. Spen welcomed me cordially but seemed to be reserving judgement.

I had not known that Eden was part-Marin, but it explained the pale eyes and hair. Spen had been Spen Fisher before training as a Thatcher. A Marin from Seabeck, Spen's hair shone bright as sunlight, lighter than Eden's and cut shorter than the Marin custom. I saw nothing of Spen in Ro, except their height.

The Cutlers had invited me to the forge for midwinter, and I might have gone had Brook's letter not told of Jay's return. Like any addict, I feared falling back into dependence. I missed Jay, as I would miss my right hand, but I was coping. Now I had made the break, it was best to stay away from temptation.

When the weather turned foul, and snow blocked many roads, we suspended our walks to the woods.

Nobody minded but the dogs. We took to spending our evenings together in Eden's rooms to share the fire and preserve our wood. The heat rose to warm my room, but it still felt chilly when we went up to bed. I would light a slow fire before we slept. Lying in bed with Fern warming my feet, the sighing of the wind around the door was our lullaby, and the ice was always thin enough to break in the morning.

Fern and I had a standing invitation to breakfast on Fundays. I knew when they were up and about from the sound of Rowan's singing, or the rumble of conversation below my floor. One morning Eden was humming a tune when I arrived. The smile that greeted me was carefree and unguarded – a burst of sunlight on a cloudy day.

I warned myself not to start getting ideas in that direction. I wouldn't make that mistake again. I busied myself laying the breakfast table while Ro recounted a classmate's misdeeds.

Eden's disapproval of Ro's amusement tightened the atmosphere. What had I been thinking of, entertaining thoughts of Eden thawing?

The dogs lay together on the fireside rug, with Bracken licking at Fern's ears. Puss was curled in a chair. How my life had changed in such a short time. My hosts' conversation registered on the edge of my consciousness – Rowan talking with a mouth full of sausage, and Eden protesting that masticating mouths should be closed. In the cottage, there had been no conversation at mealtimes. The only sound had been Ira chewing, which I would try to shut out...

"Robin! Robin, you're not listening. Do things that poison people kill dogs, too?"

"Sorry Ro, I was miles away. Yes. And sometimes things that don't hurt people can harm dogs. Cats too."

"I asked *three* times. You didn't hear me."

"Is everything all right?" Eden sounded concerned.

"Oh yes, fine. Just getting flashbacks of Ira for a moment there."

"You must miss Ira."

"Mm. Like toothache."

Rowan sniggered, and I reproached myself.

"I miss the Cutlers," I added wistfully.

Eden nodded and then became busy collecting the breakfast plates. "You should visit them."

"Yes, I will. In the spring. When the roads are dry." When the fair's on.

Eden stood at the sink now, gazing out of the window.

"You know Jay is back in Fendle?"

"Yes, I heard from Brook."

I didn't want to talk to Eden about Jay. I stood to pick up the tea towel and changed the subject. "Ash was secretive yesterday about whatever you and Logan were up to."

Eden checked, but Ro had gone out to the garden to build a snow-dog.

"I think Jess suspects we're on to them. Their house in Fendle is up for sale. I've been told the records I want to see must be out of place, but they were all there when I started investigating. Without them, we can't prove Jess paid for the Mucky Duck. It belongs to Lex Giltin."

"Only Lex? What about Geri?" There were two Giltin tarlings.

"Both worked at the Duck when it opened, but I hear the younger one is back in Fendle."

"Is there enough evidence for the Advisors then? What does Jordan think?"

"I haven't had the chance to find out. Taz tells me Jordan's been ill. I should pay a visit."

"Nothing serious, I trust."

I wasn't surprised. At first, I wondered if Jordan might be avoiding the office when I was there in the afternoons, but then Ash had confirmed they'd had no morning visits either for several days.

I preferred to discuss the Giltins. "Does Lex have a partner?"

"Yes. They settled not long before they took on the Duck. I'm told that's who runs the place. Lexi's a hard worker but not equipped for making business decisions."

"But is the partner named as part-owner? Or Jess?

"Just Lex. The Duck's been self-sufficient for a couple of years now. They may be building up another reserve for a new project. If the old rogue's set up one tarling, there's probably something planned for the other one. We can't wait much longer to find out. We'll need to move before Jess makes a run for it."

Jay

It was Funday, but we were in the workshop. Nobody was chatting. Jess had sent word that the loan, due for repayment in two weeks, would not be renewable, not even at a higher interest rate. The new inn was to be called the Hare and Hounds. Cris had spoken to its owner's agents, who regretted they were unable to advance payment for part of the order. Orders which had already been supplied took priority for payment.

I felt useless as I supervised the eldest tarlings, buffing up newly finished plate. I was finishing off the knives, but they wouldn't take long, even with half a hand. I would have liked to try that hand at jewellery, but how could I sit and fumble with scraps, surrounded by everyone else working their muscles stiff on knives and plate and kitchen tools?

Next day I went to see Jess. A cart loaded with boxes and furniture stood outside the house when I arrived. Another cart drew up while the servant went to fetch Jess. The first drove off, as more boxes and trunks were brought out to load onto the empty wagon.

"Jay Cutler! What brings you to my doorstep? Hmph."

Jess's bulk filled the doorway in a manner that didn't invite entry. I came straight out with it.

"A plea for your understanding. I was hoping I could persuade you to extend my family's loan for another week or two."

I was hoping for longer than that, but I didn't want the door shut in my face before I'd started. Jess had always seemed well disposed towards me, so might at least hear me out.

"I don't think…" Jess stepped back, and the door began to close. I brushed hair from my eyes with my right thumb and the door stopped moving. A spark flickered deep in flesh-hooded eyes.

"Oh, my dear… I heard you'd injured your hand but didn't realise how badly. Hmph, let me see."

I offered my hand. Clammy, sausage-thick fingers turned it back and forth for inspection. It was retained while Jess transferred attention to my face.

"You won't be able to work without your right hand, will you? Hmph. Not in the forge, anyway."

I didn't think it worth mentioning that I was left-handed. I let my right curl uselessly in Jess's.

"You understand then why I feel responsible for the late repayment. The forge has been working at half-strength."

"Ah yes. Kip is working at the school as well. Your little friend ran away to Tarfen. Oh dear, they are in trouble, aren't they?"

The door opened wider, and Jess relinquished my hand, stepping back to clear the entrance.

"Come in, dear. Come in."

A heavy hand landed on my shoulder, guiding me to a half-empty study. The hand released me to point to a chair where I should sit, next to a vast, polished table piled with papers which had been part-sorted into boxes.

Jess lowered into a wide chair opposite and slid the boxes aside, the better to view me across the desk.

"So, Jay, how do you plan to earn a living, hmph? I'm sure someone as… independent as you won't want to live off your family for the rest of your life."

"I'm still finding out what I can and can't do. But my family has a substantial order in hand–"

"Yes, yes. Hmph. Much as I would like to help you, my dear, and your esteemed family, I am on the cusp of a new project of my own, which will require all my resources." The treacly voice oozed regret.

"But if we don't have the money…"

"Then I'm afraid assets would be seized to pay the debt. That is the usual procedure."

We had nothing to sell to cover that amount, other than our home. I looked up, into Jess's face.

Surely not.

The piggy eyes gleamed, alive with possibilities under review. "I might, however, be able to help *you.*"

The accompanying gleam was a facial equivalent to hands rubbing together. The massive hands themselves rested on the table, as if waiting.

"I happen to know of a tavern in Tarfen that needs staff. I can put in a word for you if you're interested. Hmph The pay is basic, but I understand gratuities can be generous, and you'd be fed and housed. Are you interested?"

I recalled Jess was rumoured to have an interest in an inn at Tarfen.

"What kind of work?"

"This and that. Everyone mucks in, as it were. There would be cleaning, some bar work, food service, maybe help in the kitchen... customer service in general. Could you manage that?"

I nodded. Jess continued.

"The tavern's called the Mucky Duck. It's popular with travellers and the locals come for the entertainment – we're renowned for it – and there are other services. Singers and musicians travel from the five counties to play at the Mucky Duck."

I liked the sound of that.

And Rob was in Tarfen.

"Do you own the tavern?"

"Oh, it isn't mine, but I have influence there. You'll not be turned down if I introduce you. You can support yourself without burdening your parents."

That would be an advantage, but it didn't solve our immediate problem.

"It wouldn't help us repay the loan, though. It's due in just over a week. Not unless the Mucky Duck were willing to advance my wages."

Nor even if they were... but Jess saw I was interested.

"I would like to help, Jay. I could possibly delay my project for a week or two... if you could start work at the Duck imminently – say at the week's end? And I might look at extending the loan for a further two weeks, under the terms of the existing agreement. I believe it specifies the increased interest rate that would apply for an extension."

It did.

The new rate was exorbitant. And Jess's offers sounded too vague for my liking.

"You couldn't make it a little longer?"

"Let's say, that would depend on circumstances, hmph. In fact, if circumstance were exceptionally favourable, I might even see my way to a brief extension at the current interest rates."

I didn't dare push harder. "Won't they want to interview me?"

Now the meaty palms were rubbing together.

"I'll be in Tarfen tomorrow. I'll have a word... book you a room and arrange an interview. When can you get there?"

I didn't trust Jess, but what choice did I have?

We agreed I would arrive in three days' time. I would at least find out more about the job. And I could visit Rob while I was in Tarfen.

The loaded wagon was pulling away as the servant showed me out. On my ride home, I passed the first cart returning to the Giltin house. It can't have travelled far to unload.

Back at the forge, I found a scene similar to the one I'd just left; my family were packing. Kip and Brook were moving into the cottage and Cris's family would move back into the house. The rooms in the new extension were to be let to Sandy as guest rooms for the Barley Mow. I was to keep my room in the old house with Chris and family.

Nobody questioned me when I said I was going to look for work in Tarfen, although Cris suggested I might polish my boots first. I expected they'd be happy to have me out of the way while they moved rooms.

New Friends and Old

Robin

I never yearned to travel, as Jay did. People are the same everywhere, and Fendle was challenge enough. Scenery is earth and sky.

But I enjoyed Tarfen's busyness and different-ness. Nobody knew me. With so many people living in close proximity, I wasn't the only non-standard shape, and nobody cared.

I felt taller. Normal.

Tarfen's shops and stalls sold goods we never saw in Fendle, and I loved to wander the market. I met Mikki there one Funday, buying hot chestnuts with a Tarn called Laurel.

They seemed very comfortable together.

The Assembly buildings were the couriers' first stop on message runs from High Wenn, and we were first to hear the news from other counties.

We heard of the green shoots that appeared in scrubland bordering the wastes noonward of Wendale. Farmers were tilling parts of the waste, to try if anything else might grow there.

We heard that the Seagen had voyaged to the far side of the Shade Forest, returning with tales of towns that teemed like ants' nests, and of further lands beyond.

At home, Eden thawed as the weather froze. Sometimes, though, when we were most easy together, I sensed a sudden return to wariness. The pale eyes would blink, and the air would chill a little.

Eden was most at ease in the office, where Ash and Logan viewed their leader as an infallible machine.

Ever since Jordan had been too ill to visit, nobody questioned my presence, and I helped in the afternoons when I could – which was most of them. I had twice helped to identify causes of death and received a small consulting fee for my services.

What I was learning about Tarfen might yet be worth more than money.

I enjoyed my mornings at school but didn't want to return to teaching full time. One of the teachers, Stevie, was almost as short as me, and might have liked to take our friendship further, had Eden's introduction been less… proprietorial. I'm sure Kee and Stevie thought us closer than we were, and I had yet to find an opportunity to disabuse them.

It was best to avoid that kind of tension at work, anyway. As it was, they seemed grateful I was willing to come in for so little, but money wasn't a problem. I had discovered the Hawn Fortune.

"Fortune" proved an overstatement. Back at the cottage, I had dragged Ira's heavy oak chest across Fern's dog hatch, in case anyone came to inspect the cottage before we had time to board it over. My clumsy handling dislodged a panel at its base, and the package lay under the panel, wrapped too tightly for coins to clink when we moved the trunk.

Until I found it, I'd assumed Ira's drinking began after Sal's death, but this stash of money made me wonder if Sal hid the money for the same reason as I had hidden mine. It wasn't anything like a fortune but would be a welcome squirrel-store against unplanned expenses.

The notion flitted through my mind that I might offer it to Kip and Brook, to help tide them over.

Brook would refuse it.

Jay

We hadn't been driven to selling the horse yet – Topaz was too old to be worth selling – so I rode him to Tarfen.

I hardly noticed my surroundings on the way as I tried not to think of the day ahead of me, not wanting to build my hopes too high. Instead, I mulled over the strange prospect of Cutler's Forge without my parents there. When I left the forge, Cris and Elm had taken over our parents' room and were moving the sprogs back into the room they'd all so recently left – the room which, through my childhood, had been Ira's and Robin's.

I'd grabbed my lute and slipped away.

When I arrived at the Mucky Duck with my mind still in Fendle, I thought the lanky figure clearing tables looked familiar. When I looked again, the youngster was disappearing through a far door and my attention was claimed by a statuesque bartender greeting me by name.

I struggled to recognise Lex Giltin under a shock of beetroot-streaked hair. The formerly generous waist had thickened to vanishing point in the years since Lex left Fendle. A ferret-like character with a caustic tongue who had been tossing around instructions when I arrived must be Lexi's partner, Max.

Many of the tables were occupied in the spacious tavern. The bar dominated one wall, with a raised platform at the far end of the room. Doors labelled "Staff Only" at one side of the bar were set behind a flight of stairs.

Lex gave me a key and directions to my room, saying we'd talk tomorrow about something more permanent. The room was small, but adequate.

It hadn't been solely the forge's upheaval that set me on the road so early, and I could no longer deny my hopes for a meeting with Robin. Rob no longer answered to my searching; now I might find out why, and perhaps breach the barrier. This wasn't the kind of anticipation Storm had stirred. It was more like the longing for home after exile. Robin understood me better than anyone and had loved me anyway.

I had Rob's address and a letter from Kip, but when I reached the Assembly buildings, I found few clues to which apartments were which. Numbering was inconsistent, and I wasn't sure if I was knocking on Robin's door or someone else's. When nobody answered, I didn't wait for long.

Coming away from the square, I met Taz, who was on the way in. After fielding enquiries about my family, I learned that Rob taught in the mornings but spent most afternoons in one of the Assembly offices. With Taz's directions, I eventually found the draughty grey corridor on an upper floor which led to a room labelled, "Watchguards."

Robin wasn't there either but was expected at any minute. The two youngsters cleared me a chair and introduced themselves. Ash, round-faced and dark-haired, seemed the older while Logan was paler and spotty. Logan was on the way out to fetch lunch and offered to bring me something in as well, which I gratefully accepted. Breakfast seemed an age ago. Ash went back to filing papers into a box, stopping occasionally to decipher a spidery page and label it for easier filing. I was close enough to recognise the script.

"I never could understand how someone who writes so neatly on an easel can be so illegible on paper."

"You know each other well, then?"

"We grew up together."

Ash stretched like a cat before starting on the next pile of papers to be filed, moving aside a knife that weighed down the stack. I idly picked this up for closer inspection, and Ash glanced toward the movement. Then looked again.

"Sheeesh! What happened to your hand?"

"A horse trod on it." Ash winced. "It got infected." I was impressed how nonchalant I sounded.

It was gratifying to note that Ash seemed impressed too, but I changed the subject.

"I know about the teaching job, but what does Robin do here?"

"Helps out with the reports and filing; takes messages if we're all out; tells us the likely cause of death when we find a body, assuming it isn't immediately obvious. A slashed throat doesn't take much figuring out."

"Do you get many of those?" The knife I'd picked up from the table was hardly fit for slitting open a letter, much less a throat.

"Nah. Not really." Ash sounded disappointed.

"And Rob gets paid for this?"

"Only for the bodies. The budget doesn't allow for office work, although Eden insists we keep records. Robin does it for love."

I looked up, but Ash carried on. "We all do, really. They pay us chickenfeed."

Then lunch arrived, and my pulse steadied as I settled up with Logan.

They clearly enjoyed their work and recounted some of their more dramatic encounters as I ate my pie, until a familiar voice approached in the hall outside, together with one I didn't recognise. The door opened and Rob froze in the entrance.

No diffident browns and greys today, but a teal-green tunic, which suited Rob's colours. Those chased silver earrings were a pair I'd made: a matched pair, one in each ear. The chestnut hair looked different… longer? It shone. So did Robin, brown eyes sparkling to match a carefree smile, although now they looked uncertain.

"Jay?"

"Hello Rob."

Not the snappy dialogue I'd rehearsed.

Behind Robin stood the owner of the other voice. This must be Eden… younger than I'd imagined. Tall – taller than me, pale-skin, light hair – not golden like Sam's but fair for a Tarn. Finely sculpted features with a firm, narrow mouth. Unreadable eyes.

Robin came to life again and continued through the doorway.

In the corridor the voices had sounded relaxed and friendly, but the Tarn Rob introduced me to was reserved and formal as a funeral. Too pompous for my Robin.

Familiar, dependable Robin, who I wanted to hug – something we hadn't done since school (*why not?*). If there hadn't been all these strangers watching…

Eden said, "You and Jay will want to go and catch up. Perhaps we'll see you tomorrow, Robin."

Meeting Up

Robin

Eden said, "You and Jay will want to go and catch up. Perhaps we'll see you tomorrow."

Tomorrow? I thought. *Surely, you'll see me tonight?*

I held the office door open as Ash said, "Nice meeting you, Jay," and the maimed hand saluted in return. Brook's letter had described the damage, but it was still a shock.

Crossing the square, Jay asked after Fern and my new job. I asked after everyone at the forge and that took us to my rooms. I checked supplies, and when I turned to offer what there was to drink, Jay was behind me. Arms closed around me, and I found myself in the kind of clinch I had only dreamed of in the past. Without thinking, my arms went around Jay and, after a stunned pause, I gave myself up to the moment.

Like a reflex, my body stirred, but my mind was strangely detached. I tried to recall how I would once have felt – shooting stars, birdsong… but I'd invested too much in banishing those feelings for my guard to lower so easily. Never again would I make do with the crumbs of another failed romance. This embrace felt… needy.

But the need wasn't mine.

223

I gently disengaged and stepped back. Jay's hands slid down my arms to take my hands. "I wanted to do that as soon as I saw you."

I felt a fluttering of the link that had connected us. I might have nudged it awake, but I resisted that experiment. The grip on my left hand was tight, but not secure.

I said, "Tea. I'm making tea."

While I filled the kettle from the jug, Jay didn't settle but wandered the room, looking out of the window one minute, then fiddling with things on the mantelpiece.

"Sit down, Jay. You're making me jumpy."

Jay sat obediently in a fireside chair. "How are you finding it here? D'you think you'll come back to Fendle?"

It occurred to me that I could now visit Fendle. It would be alright.

"Tell Kip and Brook I'll visit soon," I said. "I've been so busy."

"I didn't mean for a visit, but I suppose you've answered my question."

"How are you managing, Jay? With your hand…"

"Oh, I can do most things I need to if I'm careful. Not very well, sometimes. Not in the forge, of course." The grey eyes turned bleak as stormclouds.

I spooned leaves into the teapot. "So, what brings you to Tarfen?"

Jay paused before answering.

"This and that. I'm trying to persuade Jess to extend the loan on the forge. No luck so far. But there might be a job on offer for me, and I get the impression favours might be done if I'm part of the Giltin team."

Given their history, I had doubts about Jess's employment plans for Jay who could be incredibly short-sighted at times. Maybe I should put a spoke in that particular wheel.

"I've a letter for you from Kip, by the way," Jay was saying, "but I forgot to bring it. It's at the Mucky Duck. I'll drop it in tomorrow. Is it all right to bring it to the office?"

"Of course. Make it the afternoon, though; the office may be closed till I get there." If Eden's information was correct, they would all be busy elsewhere in the morning.

"Only I got the impression your Eden might disapprove of my interruptions."

"Not *my* Eden."

"I wouldn't be so sure. I don't think your boss was pleased that I turned up."

"Not my boss, either. We're neighbours. The office sometimes has paying freelance work for me."

Jay raised an eyebrow. But I didn't discuss Jay with Eden, and I didn't intend to discuss Eden with Jay. I turned to take the kettle from the hob.

"Leave that, Rob. Come and sit, so we can talk properly."

I set the kettle on the hearth and sat in the other chair. Jay watched my face, as if trying to read it.

"I've missed you so much."

"I've missed you all, too. You're my family."

Wasn't that usually Jay's line?

"Come back to Cutler's Forge, Rob. Settle with me."

That was unexpected.

The silence stretched until Jay filled it – another first.

"Rob, we know each other better than anyone does."

I had to say something to stop this.

"We knew each other, or we thought we did. I'm not the same person now, and neither are you."

"No. That's why I'm here."

There was a promise there that plucked at a frayed heartstring. I dusted off my old dream of a life together, like revisiting a once-favourite toy.

The well-worn fantasy had worn thinner in our time apart. Once, I wouldn't have thought twice about going back, even if both Jay's hands were broken.

"I know you mean well, Jay, but you're settling for me because you can't have what you really want. That wouldn't be fair to either of us."

"I'm not settling *for* you, Rob; I want to settle *with* you. It's like a part of me is missing since you left."

"We've grown apart, Jay, as siblings do. Our links have wasted away, as siblings' do."

Could they grow again? Jay knew me better than anyone and still wanted me. Should I throw that away?

Downstairs, the dogs barked. Ro was home.

"Come down to meet Rowan and Bracken."

"Bracken?" Eyes widened.

"Fern's pup. Eden took her. She's downstairs. So's Fern; come on!"

I led the way. Jay had no choice but to follow. We were halfway down when Rowan's voice emerged into the garden.

"What have you taken? I know from the skip in your step you've got something you shouldn't."

I opened the gate and Bracken ran to it, wagging her tail and making a gift to me of a damp sock.

"Oh Robin, *thank* you." Ro took it from me. Fern had reached us by then and her tail wagged furiously at the sight of Jay.

"Jay, this is Rowan, and this…" indicating the pup, "is Bracken."

"Ah. I see." Jay's head shook, like a dog shaking off water. "It's just that I know of a 'ling called Bracken."

"Well, it's a nice name," I said. "For a dog or a 'ling"

"Parent chose it," said Ro defensively. "Have you met my parent?"

"I have. I'm Jay, by the way."

"Nice to meet you." Rowan nodded formally, and Jay returned the nod. "Would you like to come in for some tea?"

I never did finish making that tea. "Rowan, I would *love* a cup of tea."

I meant it too. Preferably with a good measure of juniper spirit!

"I must go, I'm afraid," said Jay. "I'll see you tomorrow, Rob. With Kip's letter."

Two magpies flew up from the courtyard as the gate opened. Whose omen were they? Or was there one for each of us? I hadn't seen any more magpies in Tarfen since that first day. Unless I'd been too busy to notice them.

Jay bent to kiss me goodbye. Yet another first.

As the gate closed, my thoughts churned. I should revisit the past only as memories. I couldn't go back there.

Could I?

The Mucky Duck

Jay

I had walked to the Assembly buildings from the Mucky Duck. It was further than I'd realised, but the walk back seemed longer still.

I told myself I had taken Rob by surprise, but I found little in our meeting to build hope on. I should have taken things more slowly. Robin appeared to be happy here, without me.

But Rob was the other half of me. We'd grown into each other, like trees that seeded together. I'd wanted to spread my wings a bit before settling; maybe Rob needed time to do the same.

My mood was at odds with the atmosphere in the Mucky Duck, which hummed, busy and cheerful, as I ordered my supper. The lanky one brought over a plate piled with hot meat and potatoes and paused to assess me, in no hurry to get back to the bar.

"You're the kid from Fendle, aren't you? The one Jess said to expect?"

"I was told there's a job going. Lexi said we could talk about it in the morning. Um… and mentioned a change of room?"

"Jess said to give you the room at the end of the guest landing, but it isn't free till tomorrow. It's smaller than the

228

other guest rooms, but better than the attics – not so many stairs."

The ferrety eyes skimmed over my face and a hand came out for shaking, "I'm Max, by the way. I'm Lexi's partner."

I offered my claw in return. "I don't know if Jess mentioned the hand. It doesn't stop me doing most things. I'm fine with kitchen work."

Max's hand withdrew. "If Jess is happy with it, there shouldn't be a problem. I don't know that kitchen work's what they have in mind. Jess will be here tomorrow. I've an appointment in the morning, so we'll have to talk about your duties after I've spoken to Jess. Expect to start work the day after." One eyebrow lifted. "Unless you're very good…" With a muffled snort, Max left me to my supper.

Musicians were setting up to play at one end and the room quickly filled.

After a song or two others joined the players on the dais and, as the evening progressed, singers came up from the crowd, or from behind the bar, disappearing again after their song. The stairs were busy with much to-ing and fro-ing.

The bar filled, and the music changed, and I slumped into a warm fuzzy distraction, which had as much to do with the ale as the entertainment. Songs to sing along to (for working up a thirst) gave way to singers you wanted to listen to. Beats that set your feet tapping stretched into rhythms that swayed your shoulders and stirred your hips – music that slid like a snake into your senses.

Dancers swayed around the edges of the room.

A crow with a sore throat sang of loneliness. The cawing crept into my ear and lodged there. It was a leggy crow, known to the crowd – perhaps the youngster from the bar earlier. I couldn't be sure. I'd only caught a side-glimpse of that one's face, and now people stood between my table and the platform. Some of the audience called for more, but voices stilled when the next singer began to croon, mellow and dark as moleskin. I could have listened all night.

They didn't need me singing here.

Sleep claimed me as soon as I lay on the bed, but I woke again with a sore head.

Above me, the shadows of cobwebs danced as the last embers flared in the fireplace. Muffled sounds from other rooms hinted at the services Jess hadn't detailed when describing the Duck's amenities.

I drifted again, to be jerked back to wakefulness by a sudden cry and the sound of something, or someone, falling to the floor.

The occupants of the room on the other side hadn't broken their rhythm. Across the hall, a low voice muttered, followed by an even lower reply. Elsewhere, creaks and murmurs resumed.

There was little doubt about the Mucky Duck's most profitable business.

No doubt employees were expected to participate, sooner or later. Did I still want this job?

Why was I even considering it?

But why not? I'd hardly been saving myself before Storm came along. That was over, and Robin didn't want me.

What else could I do anyway? I reckoned I'd be good at it.

At least I'd be looking after myself instead of leeching off my family. I might be able to send money home – just till they were back on their feet. We hadn't discussed terms in any detail, although Jess had said tips were good.

Suddenly, comments I'd not examined closely made more sense.

Jess was arriving tomorrow. I would start work the day after... unless I was very good.

The terms of a loan extension might be more favourable, depending on circumstances.

The guest room was better than the attics... not so many stairs.

Its convenience wasn't for my benefit.

The abstract proposition I had accepted as worthy of further investigation was suddenly uncomfortably specific.

A New Day

Jay

The sky outside lightened, and I despaired. It was tomorrow already. The other rooms were at last silent, but the chance of sleep had passed. My throat was dry, and my head still ached. I didn't think I'd drunk so much the night before.

I needed water, but my body didn't want to move. My drift back into sleep took me to water and a memory of the lake. As Storm waded from the water, arms reaching for me, the flesh thickened and wobbled... and there was Jess, drawing me closer.

I woke, sweating. My heart pounded and my head throbbed. I would get up and find a drink. A walk would clear my head.

I returned from my walk no happier, although I had at least slept in the meantime. My body had taken charge while I sat by a stream with my back against a tree, trying to think of a way out that didn't risk our home.

When I walked through the door of the Duck, Jess was standing at the bar, talking to Lex. I slipped past to the stairs without drawing their attention. Keeping my head down, I prayed to whatever shiel were listening that Lex wouldn't notice me and call out.

At the top of the stairs, I risked a glance back. Lex handed a sealed, squat bottle of something dark to Jess, who read the label with interest and nodded, setting jowls and rolls of flesh in motion. I shuddered and fled to my room.

Misgivings had been creeping in all night. This morning they tumbled over each other to be noticed. But what alternatives did I have?

If our meeting was this afternoon, I still had the morning to think about it. I abandoned the idea of breakfast and left by a back door to the stables, taking my things, since they would be moving me. I left my key in the room with a note saying, "back later," in case anyone thought I had run away. I refused to think about tonight – about anything at all.

After collecting Topaz from the stables, we set off towards the town centre, saluting Eden and Ash as I passed them in the stables' courtyard.

I wasn't riding for long before I heard dogs barking in the woods that bordered the road. The barking drew closer and people were shouting. A tall figure ran out of the trees ahead of us.

I steadied Topaz as the runner disappeared into woodland on the other side of the road. Behind, from the direction of the inn, horses crashed through undergrowth, their riders shouting directions over the barking. That cry in the night came back to me. Without thinking, I urged Topaz after the fleeing figure.

The woodland track was empty. The runner had disappeared. I reined in Topaz and heard rustling in the undergrowth that bordered the path.

"Here! On the horse."

The runner sprinted out of the bushes on long legs, which scrambled easily up behind me. "There's a brook – over that way!"

I was touched by the trust invested in me. I might have been anyone – even one of the pursuers. We rode into the stream and followed it as far as we could until the dogs sounded close. Before they appeared, we'd left the water and plunged into cover on the other side.

The shouts and the barking diminished. They were heading away from us when I stopped at the crossing of three paths. "I don't suppose you'd know where we are?"

"The Blue Shiel's that way," a hand appeared behind me, pointing along one path. "We'll be safer there."

I noted that "we" with misgiving.

In the stable yard of the Blue Shiel, my companion dropped lightly to the floor. For the first time, I could see who I'd rescued.

"It's Fin, isn't it?"

The youngster waved an acknowledgement, breathless with something that seemed suspiciously like elation. I remembered Fin as being impassive to the point of boredom.

Control was quickly regained. "Yeah. I recognised you straightaway in the Duck. What happened to the hand?"

"A horse trod on it."

"What were you doing under a horse?" Fin's voice was husky. We'd been shouting on the ride to make ourselves heard. "I expect your family won't let you go hungry because of it."

"Your voice sounds in need of a rest. Although, come to think of it, I only ever heard you grunt back at the forge."

"Yeah. I kept my head down when the parents were around. Cay's the one used to chat away, impressing everyone's families with what a polite, well-raised tarling it was. Made me squirm."

The hard-edged Tarn in front of me was no tarling now. I never had trusted this one.

"Why were they chasing you?"

"Do you want to talk about it standing here till the hunters turn up? Or shall we go in? I'm hungry."

I tried to remember what I'd been told about Fin's departure from Fendle. Something to do with burning down a barn.

Over hot food and mulled cider, I learned that I'd helped Fin evade Eden's Watchguards. Had I known sooner, I would certainly have thought twice about getting involved, but it wasn't entirely disagreeable to know we'd outfoxed Eden.

Although it wasn't Fin they'd come for.

They'd come to arrest Jess. And Jess ran, which was as good as an admission of guilt. Especially since Jess seemed to be prepared for such an eventuality, with a swift pony and trap stabled nearby.

Jess was an outlaw. I was free!

Fin didn't know what crime Jess was accused of. Heady with sudden deliverance, I hardly cared. Max had received warning, and Jess took to the back streets while Lex stalled Eden. They had sent Fin out as a decoy with the offer of a warm cape against the frost – Jess's – and the threat of Max's biggest kitchen knife for a refusal.

Jess's cape was soon discarded, but by then the dogs were committed to a hunt and had Fin's scent. Then I came along.

How might this affect the Cutler debt?

Who could advise me? I finished my drink and stood.

"I have to see someone. What will you do?" Fin shrugged. "You won't be going back to the Duck?"

Fin stood to consider this, but not for long. "Nah. Not now. Had enough of the place."

I didn't doubt it. "What about your things?"

"Got no things."

"Will you go home to Fendle?"

"Home?" The grunt was dismissive. "There's no welcome for me in Fendle."

"Probably not," I agreed. "I gather there's a torched barn to answer for."

Spindly legs shifted from one foot to the other and back again.

"That was unfortunate. I lost what little I had when the lamp went over. My things were on the other side of the flames and I had to run for my life."

"It was unfortunate for the Tillers too."

"Well, I didn't feel like waiting around to apologise. They had pitchforks!"

I took my knife from its sheath then. "Recognise that?" I held it up and Fin's brows drew together.

"Yeah, it's your knife. We saw it at the forge."

"And afterwards." The furrow deepened. "They found it at the cottage when Ira disappeared."

The bewilderment cleared. "Oh, that weren't me. Cay took it off you in the market. then went after a puppy. Must've dropped it when the old goblin turned up and chased en away."

I was unconvinced. I expect it showed.

"I didn't want your knife! I already had a good one – a small one to keep handy. Till I lost it in the fire."

It rang true. I couldn't stay debating it now. "I have to go. I've someone to see. Will you be all right?"

"How about you? Are you going back to the Mucky Duck?" The thought of facing the place again cast a shadow, but Fin was ahead of me. "We could take a room here for tonight."

I noted that "we," again. "I don't have enough money with me."

Fin looked at me blankly. But I'd not expected to be paying for a room.

My companion consulted a pocket sewn into a cloth belt. "I could manage a deposit. Come on."

We took a room. I expected Fin to have disappeared before the balance was due in the morning. But I would need more anyway, to pay for Topaz's stabling. And breakfast. Maybe Rob would help me out.

Rob, who had so often come to my rescue in the past.

I'd always taken it as my due. Could I ever make things right between us?

Day One, Ira

Fern had barked at the youngster climbing through the window, but she was used to tarlings coming to admire her litter and had no expectation of harm. Her nest smelled of milk and warm puppies. She watched closely as first one and then another were lifted for inspection.

She had seen this tarling before – roly-poly, like her pups. The youngster spoke to the puppies while comparing their features. Fern understood a lot of the words: "hide" meant a game.

"…later … say I found it."

"Found" was the end of the game, but "later" meant it might never happen.

At last, a decision was made. One wriggling pup was parted from its siblings and carried to the door.

This hadn't happened before.

Fern stepped over her nest's barrier and limped uncertainly behind the abductor. The door opened a little way, and the tarling backed through, blocking the open space with a foot. The foot pushed her back into the room, withdrawing as the door closed.

Fern whined.

From outside came a screech to muster hell's avengers.

"What do you think you're doing?"

Fern quailed.

The door slammed back, and an ungainly body fell through, rolling like a ripe apple to avoid the vigorous walking stick.

Ira filled the doorway.

The trembling thief fumbled inside its jerkin. The pup squirmed free, its frightened squeal mingling with a Tarn-yelp as metal clattered to the floor and the tarling sucked on a bleeding finger. The prized knife, lifted so smoothly from its sheath in the bustle of the marketplace, was abandoned as the child scrambled for the open window.

Fern lifted her pup by the scruff of his neck and carried him to join the others. Hen-like, she gathered them in while Ira roared across the pathway after the fugitive.

"Stop, thief! You think I don't know who you are? You don't fool me by going that way. I know where you live." The screech subsided to a cackle. "And I know a shortcut."

Fuelled by fury, the old Tarn set out towards the riverside path, indignation growing with every stiff, stubborn step.

Friends in Need

Robin

Eden had been quiet after work yesterday, even offhand. Ro seemed puzzled by the silence, so I made reassuring noises about work being busy. Eden was still uneasy at the prospect of accusing an Administrator.

Our Fendle informant had alerted the team to an unscheduled visit. They were all out watching the Duck this morning, so I had keys to let myself into the office.

On the way in, I left a bottle of damson wine at the messengers' post, addressed to Administrator Giltin at the Mucky Duck "for services rendered". The team were out on the first errands of the day, but I guessed that the reputation of the recipient would ensure its delivery, even though I had omitted to sign the direction.

When I arrived at the office, Jordan was standing outside.

"Where is everyone?"

Nice to see you too, Jordan. "They are out on Watchguard business. Can I get you tea?"

Jordan flushed, no doubt with fury at my proprietary air. I let us into the office and filled the kettle.

"Have they gone to take Jess?"

"I believe so. Sugar?"

"I hope their evidence is sound."

I sugared the cup and stirred it well. "Some of the Assembly paperwork for Fendle is missing." Jordan's dark-ringed eyes narrowed in the struggle to assess this. "But what they have tracked down shows discrepancies between taxes paid in Fendle and receipts in Tarfen."

I offered the cup, which was quickly drained and set on the table. The hand rested briefly beside it for support before pushing off towards the door. Jordan's skin glowed damply.

"Tell Ede I called in."

The Senior Administrator moved slowly, leaving the door open. A brisker step echoed on the stairs.

The cheery greeting brought no response from Jordan, but I recognised the voice before Jay entered and kissed my cheek.

"You smell of pearwood; is that new? Where is everyone? Aren't they back yet? Did they find Jess?"

How was I to answer questions about things I wasn't supposed to know? And how did Jay know?

I was saved by voices in the hallway. The team must have passed Jordan downstairs. Nobody looked happy. Eden paused on finding an outsider in the office.

"It's all right," said Jay. "I already know what happened this morning. I was there, at the stables. They sent out a decoy."

I sat. "Did Jess get away, then?"

It seems Jay had overheard Max's instructions from the stable yard but couldn't escape unseen in time to alert anyone. I asked if they had caught the decoy.

"The dogs lost the scent in the woods. Although, by then we'd realised it couldn't be Jess we were chasing. The fugitive was too nimble by far."

Eden was grey with fatigue after a restless night. "A squad of Assembly guards are on the way to Fendle, but I doubt Jess will wait around there until they arrive."

"So, what happens now?" Jay pulled out a chair and sat. "There are people in Fendle who've borrowed money from Jess. What happens to their debt if Jess is found guilty? Or not found at all?"

Eden considered the matter. "It would depend where the money came from before Jess loaned it. If it was Giltin money, the loan's still a legal contract. Repayment would be due to Jess's estate, or heirs. If it was money that came from Fendle's taxes, it ought to be repaid to the Assembly."

Jay nodded and stood. "Thanks Eden. Robin, can we talk somewhere?"

"Outside?" I guessed what was coming.

I was wrong. In the corridor, Jay asked to borrow money. "Only a few sovs? I wasn't expecting a bill for lodgings and the Blue Shiel's on the pricey side."

"It isn't cheap," I agreed. "That's where I stayed when I first arrived."

I put my head around the door to say I wouldn't be long.

It wouldn't be necessary to raid my treasure-hoard for Jay. So far, I'd had no occasion to disturb it. It occurred to me that I could make it work for me by loaning it out. I was in an excellent position to seek references. Who better than our Assembly acquaintances to vouch for the viability of my debtors? I must find out what interest I could charge... not from Jay, of course.

"I'll be back soon to return the loan."

"There's no hurry," I said. "I must visit the forge before long. I don't want to lose touch with the only family I have."

Jay looked at me in silence, as if weighing up what to say next, and then seemed to give in.

"Look, I know I've not been the most reliable person in your life, and you've no reason to trust me now, but I have changed. Don't write me off yet. Give me a chance to prove it."

Jay

I'd once thought I wasn't ready for our friendship to change, but now it was Robin who wanted to stay as we were. How could I swing the pendulum in my favour again? I weaved my way between busy market stalls, wondering how I would prove to Rob that I'd changed.

"Cheer up darlin' it may never 'appen." The wizened stallholder grinned, showing yellow eyes and matching teeth.

"I'm afraid you're right."

The Blue Shiel was quiet. I climbed the stairs to meet the strains of a love song haunting the corridor. The singing stopped as I opened the door of the room we'd taken.

"You've a croak like a lovesick frog."

I had to clear my own throat before I spoke again. "That song you sang last night... I hadn't heard it before. Where did you learn it?"

"It's mine; I made it up."

Fin had picked up my lute and was plucking experimentally at the strings. "Could you teach me to play this?"

For all I'd used it, I could've left the lute at home.

"I can tell you where your fingers go, but I can't demonstrate. We'll have to re-string it the other way if you're right-handed."

It had occurred to me I could re-string it and train my left hand to finger the chords but, so far, I hadn't the heart to try. Learning to play again as an adult wouldn't be easy, but re-stringing the lute might be a start.

Fin would have to be a quick learner. I was leaving at first light.

We didn't linger in the bar after supper. Back in the room, I packed what I could to save time tomorrow. Fin was already dozing when I went to bed – looking like a child again, with those knowing eyes no longer on constant guard. I slipped under the cover and leaned across to snuff the candle.

The body below me flinched, instantly awake. Flame smothered, I settled back, ready to sleep.

The dark shape turned towards me, and a warm hand touched my arm. "It's all right, Jay. I was just dozing. I want to…"

My free hand rested on Fin's before it moved any further. "I don't. I need to sleep, and so do you."

When I withdrew my hand, Fin's stayed on my arm. A husky whisper at my ear was unconvincingly flippant. "Don't you fancy me, then?"

I don't know why I didn't just say no.

"I have to prove to someone that I've changed my ways."

"I won't tell," came the whisper. "I'm good at keeping secrets." But the body relaxed, although the hand remained. "You learn to keep your mouth shut at the Duck if you value your tongue."

It felt like a confidence, of sorts.

It seemed a fair exchange to tell how I lost my fingers, which inevitably included something of Storm.

I murmured on, after the hand slipped from my arm and I thought my listener asleep. When I stopped, the room was silent. Not for long.

"I only flinched because I slept. I never flinched at the Duck. Not once. Customers don't like it." The burning wood crackled in the grate. "Except for those who do, and I wouldn't give them the satisfaction."

I recalled the bump in the night. "Were there many of those?"

"Nah … Max would ban them. Bad for business to have the staff limping around with bruises. It's a well-run house as such places go."

"And how would you know how they go?"

"I listen."

The whisper, sent to the ceiling, was as flat and as expressionless as the face that had inspected my knife in the workshop. The image arose of Jess's face with its hungry anticipation and a chill shuddered through me to my toes.

"How did you bear it?"

I felt the shrug beside me under the covers. "They're only using a shell. They don't reach me… inside. I expect it's different if you've known the real thing."

Did I hear awe in the sleepy whisper? Or might it have been scorn? It's difficult to tell from a whisper. At least we'd cleared the air between us.

A final drowsy murmur carried Fin into sleep. "But if you change your mind…"

Robin

I didn't return to the office. I had to think.

Jay's change of heart had caught me unprepared. I had no intention of going back to the way things had been and the muppet I was. But if I stayed in Tarfen, was I jumping out of the kettle onto the coals? I had to be self-supportive – practically and emotionally.

I went down to collect Fern and met Rowan coming in from school.

"Robin, I heard you might go back to Fendle." It was an accusation.

"Really? Where did you hear that?"

"Last night. Before you came down." Ro's eyes widened. "But I wasn't to say anything."

"I won't tell." I smiled. "I'm not going anywhere, sweetheart, except to visit. I live here now."

Rowan nodded firmly, in confirmation of a truth never really doubted.

Voices below signalled Eden's return home as I fed Fern. A boiled kettle later, there was a knock at my door.

"Ro wants to know if you're coming down to join us this evening."

"Of course. I've bread that needs toasting if we want a late snack."

Eden sat. "And will you be going home to Fendle soon?"

"To visit. I don't have a home in Fendle. Someone else is living in the cottage now."

Eden picked dog-hairs from the arm of the chair. "And Jay?"

"Jay's going home tomorrow."

Pale eyes met mine, with unspoken questions. Was I reading this right? Had Eden stepped back – as I had – out of reluctance to make do with crumbs? Or was I wish-thinking again? Back then, I'd pushed Jay too soon. I didn't want to send this timid deer running for cover. Those straight, firm lips offered no clues.

How might they feel on mine?

When they did finally part, I'd almost forgotten to listen.

"You'll be staying in Tarfen, then?"

"I like it here."

I waited, to be rewarded with a dawning smile that would warm toast. Mine widened in response, till it was too wide to stay crooked. Eden stood. My skin prickled with anticipation.

"I'd better go, or Rowan will wonder where I've got to."

You can't just leave... but the door was opening. "See you in a while. Don't keep us waiting too long."

What was that supposed to mean? Or wasn't it supposed to mean anything? I shouldn't count my fruit before the flowers set.

Wouldn't Jordan disapprove!

I smiled again. I could deal with Jordan.

Back Home

Jay

We settled the bill and left the tavern together. Outside, I stopped and checked that my pack was securely fastened.

"Um… my family doesn't know everything… about the breakup with Storm. I'd sooner you didn't tell anyone. I'm trying to forget about it."

"Of course."

I gave the strap one last tug. "Worst day of my life."

"You've led a sheltered life then." Fin was assessing the rain clouds. Unruly hair ruffled like feathers in the wind.

I asked, "Where will you go now?" The eyes that met mine were blank.

What else could I say? "I suppose you can come with me…"

The sharp nose wrinkled in distaste. "Nah, I won't go back to Fendle."

"Well, if you're not going back to the Duck either, where are you going to stay tonight?"

The inn sign creaked.

I sighed.

"You can come back with me for tonight. Nobody needs to know you're in Fendle. We'll set you up with some clothes and a blanket or two, maybe find a delivery wagon to take you out of the area. Topaz can't carry us both, though. You'll have to walk some of the way."

But Topaz was a sturdy workhorse, and there was no spare flesh on Fin's bones. I hadn't regained weight since the fever, so Fin rode part of the way behind me and we walked for part of it. I fancied there was relief behind the chatter as Fin's guard relaxed.

"When I left home, I planned to travel, but I had to stop and earn some money after I lost my stuff. I couldn't feed myself without a knife for hunting and gutting. There'll be plenty of casual work coming up now soon, seedtime to harvest. Now I know I can earn some coins singing, I might fall in with a travelling band in need of a voice."

The future having been settled, the past was re-examined.

"You fascinated everyone at school, you know. Even the teacher used to light up when you came to meet 'n."

As if it had been years since Fin left, instead of weeks.

"And your family – they seemed to actually like each other. We'd walk through that yard, and hope some of the luck might rub off on us. I wanted to be you… Course, you were a cocky crow back then." Now things were getting over-familiar. "You've gone a bit boring since. I suppose it comes with being older."

When words finally presented themselves, I found my mouth already open.

"Well, since I'm too old to run, and we want to get home before dark, I'm getting back on the horse, and you can jog alongside."

I mounted Topaz and urged him to a gentle canter, which Fin had to match, and that silenced the twittering.

Later we slowed to a walk, and I was irked to find the pace hadn't wearied the urchin. Instead, Fin seemed energised by the run. The breathless laugh that greeted my drop in pace soon settled to regular breathing. Before long, a marching song was marking our steps.

I stopped to pull the singer up behind me and urged on the horse. The next song was a hunting song, which I had a good harmony for, so I joined in. It felt good to be singing again.

We arrived home late afternoon. Daylight was stretching a little further each day, and it wasn't yet dusk. I led Topaz into the stable, where the scruffy mutt's tail wagged at me, sending straw flying from his nest. He eyed Fin warily and didn't come to greet us. I nodded towards the dog.

"He doesn't like you."

"I'm not too keen on him, either. He bit me."

Disbelief must have shown on my face because Fin pushed back a sleeve to show me the scar.

"What did you do to earn that?"

"I did sit on him," Fin admitted. "A big ginger cat shot between my legs and he was under my feet."

It explained why the dog, at least, hadn't come to greet me.

Lamps were burning in the workshop. Through the windows I saw everyone gathered there... and Danni, too. They suspended their discussion to greet us and acknowledged Fin's presence with bemused nods.

For my benefit, Danni began again. The Wysmith's order was ready for the new inn's stables, but the agent had sent regrets. They no longer represented the Hare and Hounds. Communications should be directed to the owner, Geri Giltin.

They had found Geri clearing debris from the completed rooms of the inn between swigs from a stubby, dark bottle. There was no sign of any builders.

Builders had stopped work, due to there being no money to pay them… or the Wysmiths, or anyone else. Jess had gone, taking the money put aside for the Hare and Hounds and anything of value that was portable.

Geri had welcomed the break from clearing and assured them that everyone would receive full payment when the Giltin house was sold. In the meantime, there was a loan due for repayment that would fund a substantial downpayment on what the Hare and Hounds needed to open for business.

But nobody felt inclined to part with their goods on a promise.

"The poor beggar did look uncomfortable," said Danni. "After all, you can't help what your parents get up to."

A grunt from behind me backed this up. "Geri seemed a right 'un at the Duck – not the sharpest blade on the knife belt and a bit odd, but never nasty. Helped out sometimes… remembered to tip before leaving." Fin subsided into thought.

None of them knew why Jess had disappeared without warning, so I told them what I had learned. "Jess is on the run from the Guards. Robin said it was something to do with Fendle's taxes."

"Won't the Assembly seize the house then?" asked Elm.

Brook thought not. "Gil's half of the house was left to Lex and Geri." Jess's partner, Gil, had died four years earlier. "The moneylending business is theirs too, although Jess ran it. Gil's legacy founded it."

My new-sprung hope wilted. We were still in debt to the Giltins.

Danni spoke up again. "If you still need help, they said I can come and give you a hand tomorrow. Except…"

Except there was no hurry to finish the order if we wouldn't be paid for it.

"And Geri plans to call in our loan to pay the Wysmiths." So much for my hopes of getting the loan extended.

"Will the Assembly take the Hare and Hounds for the taxes owed?" asked Elm.

"Sandy says Geri's registered as owner," Brook said, "and the building's almost finished now. No child of Jess will leave a place standing empty when it could be making money. And it can't open for business without cutlery or plate or kitchen tools. Surely, we can barter with some of the goods to pay off the loan."

Cris turned to Danni. "Thanks for the offer of help, pet. We can certainly use your help if we're going to carry on with this."

"Magic! I'm looking forward to it."

"We'll need to talk to Geri first. Then one of us will come over and see you."

I'd forgotten Fin until a voice behind my ear murmured. "What'll you do if Geri has to give up the inn and can't buy your stuff?"

"Shiel knows! It'd take a lifetime to sell this much tableware to villagers who eat off wood platters and cut their meat with sheath knives."

Brook took off the heavy forge apron. "Cris is right. We can't make decisions till we've spoken to Geri. We've done enough for today. I think we're all due some time off. Jay – and Fin – come to the cottage for dinner. Sort yourselves out and follow us over."

Retaliation

Jay

In my room, I found garments that would fit Fin, loosely speaking, and we changed out of our travelling clothes.

The stray dog followed me whenever I emerged into the yard. By the time he'd followed us to School Lodge, he'd decided Fin wasn't a threat, but he didn't come inside when Pickle barked at our approach. It was getting dark by then.

Inside, I bent to rub Pickle's ears, and Fin joined me, gingerly stroking the back of her head. Pictures from home hung on the cottage walls. I recognised the covers on the seats, but other than that my parents had brought little from Cutler's Forge. The small cottage still seemed over-furnished.

Kip's cat, Marmalade, had apparently resisted all attempts to relocate him, stubbornly stalking back along the lane to Cutler's Forge each time he escaped the cottage.

The fire crackled cheerfully. The welcome was equally warm, but my small cloud had followed us in, and Fin reverted to grunts. Brook, resisting all efforts to talk about the order, wanted to hear about Tarfen.

"How was Robin? Did you remember Kip's letter?"

"Rob's fine, looking well."

"And Bracken? Does she look like Pickle?"

"Pretty much. Smaller. Not so much brown."

"Did you see Taz?"

My responses grew shorter; I'd be mute as Fin by the end of the evening. Kip swooped. "Are you all right, Jay? What happened in Tarfen?"

"I'm fine, just not feeling talkative tonight. I've caught it off this one," indicating Fin, who was playing tug with Pickle over a strip of rabbit fur. A snort acknowledged my remark as the game continued. To keep Kip happy, I told them about how we'd met up and the decoy hunt.

Pickle barked for attention, annoyed that her game had been abandoned. Fin was staring ahead at nothing, every sense alert. As we stopped talking we all heard it... angry voices out on the Fendle road. They grew louder as they turned into the lane.

Flickers of torchlight played around the window's shutter, as a group of villagers swarmed through the gate, calling for Fin.

It was my fault. "I'm sorry Fin; I should've warned Danni not to spread it about that you were back."

Brook had gone to the door but thought better of opening it when a stone thumped against the wood. I gestured Fin out of sight as Kip called from the window.

"Dane Tiller, stop that now!"

Brook bolted the door and came to join us at the window. The scrawny champion at the front of the crowd struggled to shout louder than the general uproar.

"We've no argument with the Cutlers. We know Fin Hartwood's in there."

The Tiller family was at the forefront of the mob, spread out like picket fencing as others gathered behind them. The Elvers were there too but kept to the back of the swarm. Cay Elver was last to shuffle through the gate. There were no Hartwoods.

The voice that had regulated my childhood and now commanded a classroom rang out with authority.

"Come to Cutler's Forge tomorrow then. Just the two of you, not the entire village. You can talk to Fin there."

"I ain't that stupid, Kip Cutler! Sneaky minx'll be halfway to Seacrag by then."

I left the window and beckoned Fin to the back of the cottage where Ira's trunk hid the rough wood that now secured Fern's former escape flap.

"You need to get out of here. Help me pull this out of the way. While they're all at the front, you can get away through the trees at the back."

Kip saw what we were doing and came with fire irons to lever the wood away from the wall. Fin disappeared out to the pup's former exercise pen and hopped over its low fence while we pulled the chest back to cover the hole.

A smell of burning wood grew stronger, and I turned to see smoke billowing under the door. It rolled across the floor, rising into the room, and flames appeared at the bottom of the door. Kip tried to smother them with a blanket, but they quickly took hold of the dry wood. Soon the wall beside the door was smouldering.

Outside, the cries had changed to alarm. People near the door backed away, and some ran to the pump, calling for buckets. Dane stepped back from the window, holding the torch high and away from the cottage.

"Come on, you'll have to come out now. Bring that fire-raiser with you, or leave 'n in there to burn. 'S all the same to us."

Flames lit the garden. Behind the mob, a dark shadow left the cover of the house, sprinted to the open gate, and turned. An impossibly long arm stretched backwards… and pitched.

A length of wood, scavenged from Fern's enclosure, sailed towards the mob. Cay yelped, spinning to find the culprit, and Fin skipped through the gate towards the school. Half the pack took up the chase and Fin fled into the trees.

Others stayed to tackle the fire. Kip helped Brook climb through the window as I took both jugs of water to the burning door, but my water had no effect, and I couldn't reach the bolt through the flames. Kip passed Pickle through the window and clambered out to safety.

"Jay, come on. Out. Now!"

A tremor stole much of the authority from the order. All I'd ever brought Kip was worry and problems.

Brook's call was steadier. "There's nothing you can do in there, lambkin. Come on out."

No-one had called me that since I was seven. I hoped Fin was out of earshot.

Dane Tiller had been too intent on us to notice Fin's antics and was trying to peer through the window to see who was inside. Climbing out, I swept aside the bony carcass like a cobweb.

"Oi, watch it! Throwin' yer weight around as usual, Jay Cutler."

"Me! *I'm* throwing my weight around… You bring a mob here to bully a kid who's barely out of school… what were you planning? A lynching?"

"Course not!" The denial wavered as Dane backed away. "We'd take 'n to Hartwoods, for a warning. Someone oughter pay for my barn."

"A warning!"

Dane backed away into the person behind. I took a breath and shook my head. What was the point? Instead, I pointed to the flames spreading towards us.

"I hope you can afford to pay the Administration for this, then."

"Me? I didn't fire it. It's me that's owed! That tramp burned my barn… and a winter's hay."

A challenge thundered from the lane.

"That old barn was falling down, anyway! And your neighbours have given you enough hay to serve your scraggy beasts till harvest."

Then Annis Reaper was at the gate. "You have wood to rebuild too, if you and your idle clan could stir yourselves to get on with it."

Cris vaulted the fence, which was an impressive feat, given my sibling's expanding bulk. A group of villagers followed Annis through the gate: Sandy, Mikki, Sen Fletcher, Rob…

Rob? What was Robin doing here? I'd sensed no presence, but my spirits rose.

Then the group set to fighting the fire and faces merged into shadows.

We did what we could, but soon realised we were wasting our efforts. I hoped the Cutlers wouldn't be expected to replace the cottage, but even that thought couldn't dampen a surge of optimism. I looked around for Rob.

The Tillers had retreated to the gate, but Sen Fletcher and four of the Barley Mow regulars blocked their way. The pack who'd taken off after Fin was trickling back along the lane, trying to slip past unnoticed.

Annis confronted Dane Tiller. "Did you torch this?"

Dane's head shook frantically, but it was Brook who answered. "No, Dane was at the window when it caught. I

257

don't know about the others, though. They were all mooing around like skittery cows out there. It might have been an accident."

Annis eyed the subdued vigilantes as if surveying a crop of blighted potatoes.

Sen Fletcher said, "The usual ringleaders aren't here…" The shrill voice rose to carry across the fence. "…But I see their neighbours are."

The Elvers faltered as they slunk past the gate. Annis's reply was less strident. "I understand the Hartwoods are keeping a low profile these days. Young Fin's been an embarrassment to them, one way or another."

"That's one blessing then."

We'd backed away from the fire as far as the fence. I searched again for Robin as people trailed past the gate. Sen's voice rose again for the benefit of the departing troublemakers.

"If nobody knows who started the fire, I reckon Taz'll have to put everyone's taxes up to pay for a new school lodge."

"Well, we can't live here now." Kip's voice came from behind me. "We'll have to move back into the new rooms."

They'd probably be called "the new rooms" till the sprogs had sprogs of their own.

Sandy spoke up. "They're let for the week, but I've a room available in the Barley Mow till they're free."

"We can all have breakfast together," said Rob, emerging from the smoke.

Kip was delighted. "Robin! What are you doing here?"

Rob's eyes shone in the fire's light. "I'm staying at the Barley Mow. Cris came for help when the mob passed Cutler's Forge heading this way."

"Why didn't you let us know you were coming?"

"It was a last-minute decision. Mikki was bringing a wagon from Tarfen today, so I grabbed a free ride. I'd only just arrived at the Barley Mow when Cris appeared."

"Are you here to stay?" I could only hope.

"I'd come for Ira's chest, but it looks as if I won't be needing Mikki's wagon to go back home."

Home?

All heads had turned to the burning cottage as Rob continued. "Eden and I have applied for a bigger apartment. We're settling together."

My family gathered around in celebration while I rearranged these words in my head, trying to make them mean something different.

"But…" I stammered. "Yesterday…"

"I know. I'm still in a haze myself. It happened so quickly. You were right about Eden, after all. I hadn't let myself believe it."

I could find no words. I wasn't even sure what I wanted to say, but Kip and Brook made up for my silence with their congratulations. Brook asked if one would take the other's name.

"We thought not. We want to share a name, but I have no love for my family name and neither of us are thatchers. We thought Hawk would be a better match than Hawn for what we do now."

I'd thought Eden looked more stork than hawk, but Kip and Brook were both nodding approval.

I scanned the trees for a Fin-sized shadow as we left, but was distracted, as was everyone, by the collapse of the cottage roof. Sparks flew; it was quite spectacular.

As we watched, I took stock. Debt due next week; no payment in prospect, even if we'd finished the order; no stock that we could sell quickly; and now no rent coming in either.

That was one thing I could help with.

"You can rent out my room. I'm going travelling. Always wanted to travel, didn't I?"

Kip began to object, but I overrode the protest.

"I'll take some tableware with me and try to get some orders, and I'll send the money back for what I sell."

"Let's talk to Geri before we start selling stuff off," said Brook, ever the optimist.

"We'll talk about it tomorrow." I agreed. There was no harm in humouring them tonight.

I would take myself out of their way and there would be one less mouth to feed. As we walked back to the forge, the scruffy crossbreed came out to meet me.

Buying Time

Jay

I lay in bed and surveyed my room. For tonight, it was still my room. The mutt lay curled at the end of the bed on a heap of my clothes. How did he get in?

Fin had turned up at the forge last night but was already up and gone, having first picked through my shirts for a clean one. I started to fold them again.

As I moved yesterday's cast-offs out of the way, a slender coin-shape fell to the floor, threaded with a plaited leather necklet. I'd last seen it around the neck of Sen Fletcher. I'd thought it showy. Silver's my metal. Silver's lucky. This was gold and worth a Chief's ransom.

Brook was in the kitchen. "Do you want some breakfast? There are eggs and the bread's fresh."

"I'll make it. Can you give this to Sen? I think it's Sen's. It must have fallen off last night. I found it in the lane, but they'd gone."

Brook pocketed the necklet. "Fin left early. Didn't say where. I'm off to see if there's anything to salvage from the cottage. I doubt I'll be gone long."

I filled the kettle and selected my eggs. The dog sat nearby, looking hopeful.

Nobody was working, so I had the workshop to myself. The fires were cold. I warmed my hands at the lamp on my workbench before taking the whetstone to my knife.

The door opened. After a pause, Brook entered and picked up a flask of Rob's silver-tonic on the way to my bench. "That handle could do with a drop of this."

The etching on it had yellowed. "When I've sharpened it."

"So could your earrings."

When I glanced up, Brook's back was turned. I carried on sharpening. Next I knew, a stool was drawn up to the other side of the workbench.

"Your ears'll turn green."

I sighed and removed the offending hoops to examine them. I looked up to meet Brook's scrutiny. "Are they green?"

Brook inspected each earlobe. "Not yet. It'll do no harm to clean them, though."

I dipped a clean scrap of rag in the jug of water and rubbed at each ear lobe. Taking the rings from what was left of my fingers, I dropped them with the earrings into a small dish and covered them with the solution before returning to my blade.

"Are you planning to leave soon?"

"Tomorrow. I can sleep in the home-room if you need the bed."

"No, Sandy can put us up a couple more nights."

A crust on one ring caught my eye. I stopped sharpening to scratch it free and pushed the ring back under the liquid.

"Keep in touch, won't you? Kip's worried about you."

"You're not, then?"

Brook met my eye. "Parents worry. It's what we're for."

I dipped a rag in the dish of cleaner and applied it to the knife's handle.

"Write." Brook stood and replaced the stool at its proper workbench. "Take Topaz."

I looked up. "Are you sure?"

Brook shrugged. "One less mouth to feed."

Before the door closed again, I remembered to say, "Thanks, Brook."

Back in my room, I chose a clean tunic, then decided to change all my clothes. Afterwards, I sat on the bed and took my knife from its sheath to test the blade again. I hardly felt its draw, but a fine red line appeared on my thumb.

"Will you show me how to sharpen mine like that?"

From the doorway, Fin's unblinking stare moved from my hands to my eyes. The mutt edged through the door before it closed.

I'd have expected a hunter could hone a blade as well as a knifesmith.

"I thought you'd gone," I said.

"I've been home." I raised my eyebrows. "They've donated a horse. They seem keen to get rid of me."

"A horse?"

"Don't get excited; it's only Chancer. He's older than I am."

"Still. Better than walking."

I slipped the knife back in its sheath and picked up the lute.

Geri came to the forge around lunchtime, but found it empty so called at the house. Elm went to find our parents while Cris made tea for everyone and laid out cheese and oat bread.

Geri looked ill and didn't eat but kept wincing as if punched in that solid stomach. The youngest of the Giltins wasn't good at small talk and stood silent at the living room window until everyone had arrived. Seen from behind, it might have been a younger Jess standing there, before that solid flesh slackened into flab.

Fin had disappeared into the bedroom. The rest of us sat around the table. Geri got straight to the point.

"Your loan is due in a few days. I've brought the agreement."

Brook replied. "We'd like to extend it, if we can."

Geri trundled on as if no-one had spoken.

"I need to open the Hare and Hounds to get some money coming in. To do that, I need plate and cutlery and kitchen tools and saddlery. I can't pay for any of it until the Cutlers' loan is repaid." No extension then. "And you can't repay the loan till *I've* paid *you* for what I ordered. Am I right?"

Brook looked bemused. Kip looked interested. Heads nodded.

A sharp rap at the door coincided with it opening on Beck Wysmith, Brook's cousin. Beck greeted Geri first. "Ah, you're here!"

Beck nodded at Brook. "I reckoned you'd want to know what I thought of Geri's proposal."

"We haven't heard it yet."

Beck dragged another chair to the table. "Carry on, then."

Geri didn't wait for Beck to be seated. "You Cutlers owe me a hundred sovs plus interest. That makes a hundred and twenty if you pay it back now." The fact that we couldn't didn't bear repeating. "Now, I owe Wysmith's Forge one-seventy, and Cutler's Forge'll be due three hundred for the full order." Another pause for nods all around. "Right. The inn's nearly finished, but I need to start pulling customers in now, so's I can pay you all sooner."

Would the Hare and Hounds be another Mucky Duck? Geri had a sharper edge than Lex.

"Right now, I could open up the bar and the kitchen, and a few guest rooms." A gasp interrupted the flow, and Geri turned white, but waved away Brook's concern. "It's just a stomach upset."

If Geri was doing the cooking, this might not bode well for the Hare and Hounds' future customers. Geri ploughed on.

"So… this is my proposal. If each forge were to let me have a third of the goods you've got for me, I'll write off the Cutlers' loan and tear up the agreement, and you'd owe the money to the Wysmiths. You can decide between yourselves how Brook pays Beck for the goods." Eyes moved from one to the other, trying to gauge how this was being received. "I'll take the rest of the goods as soon as I can pay for them. When we've got a buyer for the house."

Geri didn't look well enough to open any time soon, but Kip was busy working this out.

"You'll be getting nearly a hundred and sixty sovs-worth of goods for a debt of a hundred and twenty!"

Geri nodded. "And you'll owe sixty to your cousin."

"Which we can't pay," said Cris.

"Interest free." Geri added.

"No!" Brook was thinking it over. "No, we'd pay interest. What do you think of this, Beck? I don't see how it helps you at all."

"Nor did we. But you're family, and you're in trouble. And I trust you to pay us more than I trust this crook."

"We will pay interest," Kip said. "But not Jess's rates."

We all avoided mentioning the extended deadline we'd need – ideally with no penalty in the form of higher interest. It was as if the room was holding its breath while we looked for a catch.

"You must settle with the Wysmiths first for the remainder," said Brook. "Before you pay us."

Geri argued the inn needed kitchen equipment more than stabling gear. Nobody mentioned we hadn't completed the work yet.

Geri produced a new agreement for the cousins to sign. Brook tore up the old loan papers and fed them to the fire.

As Geri left, Fin was at the stable door and saluted. Geri's answering nod was brief. Fin watched until the horse was out of sight and then came over.

I asked, "How well do you know Geri?"

Fin's mouth twitched. "Well enough. I doubt our paths are likely to cross again soon, though."

"Have they crossed lately?" Fin's eyebrows queried my meaning. "Since Tarfen?"

The hovering grin widened. "Didn't I mention? I dropped around for a chat last night."

Indoors, Elm was opening a bottle of sloe wine, chattering happily.

"If they open up with our stuff, they'll have to buy the rest from us. They want it all matching." One feature that had won us the order was the motif Kip had designed for the inn.

Brook looked younger.

"I don't like owing anyone, but if I have to, I'd rather it's you."

Beck shrugged and took the drink Elm offered.

"We've shifted some of the stock that's cluttering up the place, and it makes sense to help Geri get the place running. We'll all get paid sooner."

And Brook would feel indebted long after the money's repaid…

But I didn't want to prick anyone's bubble with my cynicism.

I took myself out to the workshop. The mutt was waiting for me, sprawled across the threshold.

The sun was breaking through the haze that had hung around the yard all morning. Across the way, white mists rolled over the ploughed soil, and tiny field birds burbled dementedly in the emerging warmth. Heaven knows where they'd been through winter, but birds are survivors. Spring was on the way.

I would be somewhere else.

I found tallow in the workshop to clean my filthy boots.

My brain works better with my hands busy. It seemed my family was surviving the mess I'd made – despite my efforts rather than because of them. I might not be so lucky in future, but at least now my blunders wouldn't hurt my family.

When my boots were polished to a shine, I put them on and admired the transformation. I was ready to celebrate my family's reprieve.

Beck had gone when I returned to the house, and the tarlings were home from school. Fin perched on a stool at the kitchen worktop while Brook and Kip sat at the table. Both looked drained.

I set a sealed pot of Rob's silver-tonic in front of them.

"Can I take this?"

"Are you still going then?" Kip looked worried. "I thought maybe…"

I nodded. "Tomorrow."

Kip's smile was hesitant. "I know you always wanted to travel, but are you sure you're fit? Doesn't your hand still hurt?"

I shrugged one shoulder. "Mustn't grumble."

Moving On

Robin

No regrets. It's good to be back in Tarfen.

In Fendle, I appreciated being the one to set the pace for a change, while Jay floundered. Now I have made that mental break from my fixation on a future with Jay, I can stand back and see things more clearly.

I was so desperate to belong.

Jay came with a proper family – a cocoon of Cutlers to keep me safe. The forge insulated me from the stares and the whispers and Ira.

I will always be fond of Jay, but I have emerged from my cocoon, and I have space to spread my wings.

Here in Tarfen, nobody sees me as deformed, thanks to careful tailoring and good posture. Already I have my circle of influence, and it is growing.

Fendle will need a new Administrator to replace Jess and I expect Taz will take the opportunity to stand down as well. I'm rooting for Annis Reaper, but the Fletchers will push for another of their own as Taz's replacement.

But wouldn't Kip make a good Minstrer? I wonder if Tarfen can influence the decision.

The only fly in the salve of Tarfen is Jordan, but not for much longer. When Eden and I announced we would be settling together, the lads cheered but Jordan almost collapsed.

It takes little these days to overwhelm Jordan. I am almost tempted to hurry things along, but that would be reckless.

And, in this case, the sooner is not necessarily the better. Eden is more than ready to step into the shoes of a Senior Administrator but may yet take a little persuading. The Watchguards would then need a replacement operational Administrator, and it's true that neither of the lads are yet ready to take over Eden's role.

But I am.

Fin

From outside, Cutler's Forge looked just the same. It felt as if I'd been away longer that I had, but Fendle takes time to forget.

Brook looked older. Wiser…? That old Tarn weren't stupid to start with.

The other one means well, but Jay's Kip lives in a simple world – all black and white – and I'm shelved on the darker side.

"You're not planning to pursue your new career any further then?"

"Depends," I said, "on how hungry I get. It's easy money."

"Is it?" asked Kip, not expecting an answer.

Didn't get one, anyway.

Kip tries to read your thoughts, but the other one reads your soul. Brook's eyes didn't register disapproval, nor pity. But they sought something in mine. They'll find no answer there, but they're welcome to try.

I was being measured up to look after their lambkin, although I can't see why I should be responsible for Jay. I know it were meant well, but I hadn't needed rescuing from that bunch of part-time hunters and their house dogs.

But back when Jay had the knife out that morning in the bedroom... well, I've wondered if that were what Kip were afraid of.

Maybe if the Watchguards'd come a day later for Jess they might both have had cause to worry. A comfy upbringing doesn't make for resilience. I'd overheard Lex telling Max about the new tom Jess'd wished on 'em. But I haven't told Jay that.

The gold piece were gone when I went back to the bedroom. Careless of me, that were, leaving it there. I didn't take it from Sen – though I could've, easily. I found it by the gate when they'd gone. Not that anyone'd believe me. They've all made up their minds about me. They won't change 'em now.

That Hare and Hounds hotel won't be ready to open by midwinter with Geri still weak as a kitten with guts ache. I took Cay around there to help out with the donkey work. With luck it might lead to a proper job when the hotel opens.

After this settling at the weekend in Tarfen, the plan is to move on to Wendale. Jay goes on about forests and mountains – trying to convince one of us, I think – but I don't mind flat fields and big skies. I like Tarn's open-ness.

It's a shame its people in't the same. Wherever you go, it's folks that'll spoil it for you.

After the settling, we didn't hang around at Tarfen. We passed through overnight and reached the other side as dawn was breaking. We came to a whole bunch of magpies tormenting some other bird. The mutt ran and scattered them before we got there, but Jay was trying to count them as they flew off, like my parents used to. Superstitious hogwash.

Jay seemed happy with the five I said I'd counted anyway. Five for silver.

Later that morning, we met up with a group of players on the road. I've sung with them before. They were heading for one of the border villages where they're booked for a settling.

We were singing on the road when they caught up to us, so we'll be singing together on Freeday for some of the songs. It's a good sound – Jay's clear harmony behind my growl. We might come away with some coins… but whatever the earnings it'll mean a good feed and a nice warm barn to sleep in for a night or two.

That mutt makes a good footwarmer on a cold night, even though he can't seem to make up his mind whose feet he's going to warm. He'll have to decide when we go our separate ways. Jay didn't think he'd still be with us this far from Fendle. I doubt he'd find his way back now. We ought to give him a name if he's staying.

Maybe he wants to see the sea too. I do. I've heard it flows backwards and forwards, not just one way like the river. They say that sailing on it is like flying on water. Sometimes I dream I'm flying…

No-one's mentioned Scarth.

Reviews always appreciated

If you enjoyed this story, please leave a review
at Amazon or Goodreads

About Cathy

Cathy Cade is a former librarian who enjoys solving puzzles. She began writing in retirement to exercise the other side of her brain.

She lives with her dogs across a fence from London's Epping Forest.

Cathy's writing has been published in various collections online and in print, including *Scribble*, *Best of British*, *SevenDays*, *The Fens*, *Flash Fiction Magazine*, *To Hull and Back Short Story Anthology 2018*, and *Fractured Fiction Anthology II*. Her stories and verses can also be found in collections from the Whittlesey Wordsmiths writers' group.

Cathy's books, *The Godmother*, *Witch Way, and other ambiguous stories*, *A Year Before Christmas*, and *Pond People* are available from Amazon.

Find Cathy online at **cathy-cade.com**

Other Books By Cathy

Euphemia Ffinch, godmother to Lucinda Eleanor, has been travelling since she retired as nanny to the Regalian royal family.

Buttons the dog has lived in the basement with Cindy since his master died. Cindy's stepmother treats her as a servant and is no dog lover.

Prince Alfred of Regalia is dreading his birthday ball. His stutter gets worse in company and the daughters of the nobility look down on him; they are all taller than he is. He'd rather invite the girl he met online.

Euphemia learns that Cindy's father has died. Her intuition tells her she is needed back in Regalia. But Cindy hasn't read the fairy tales and has plans of her own.
Somebody has plans for Euphemia too, and Buttons isn't sure he has a future to plan for.

"A lovely short story with some humour and twists to the plot that makes it a pleasure to read." – Sally Cronin

Short Stories with a question…

Witch Way

and other ambiguous stories

Cathy Cade

Sixteen stories, some placed or shortlisted in competitions. Add a flash or two, some verse, and a motley collection of characters who aren't all they seem – or are they? You decide.

Meet mirlings and brownies, a citizen of Pompeii, an unsettled soul, a misguided confidante, an unlikely Samaritan, a trainee mortician, and a witch... or not.

"Have re-read it several times" Goodreads; *"An eclectic collection ... varied and entertaining"*, Sally Cronin; *"A little gem of a collection"*; *"had me on the edge of my seat ... Definitely worth a read"*, Amazon review.

A Year
Before Christmas

by

Cathy Cade

Emmie Elf works hard, running errands and sweeping our reindeer stalls, but Santa's newest recruit finds herself grounded on the biggest night of the year.

Can Emmie get airborne in time for next Christmas Eve?

"*Would make a great stocking-stuffer gift,*" John Spiers. "*A lovely story*", Amazon review.

Pond People

Mirlings live in the fishpond

Cathy Cade

Mirlings live in the garden fishpond.

When Molly meets newcomer Flash, their dislike is mutual. But it becomes difficult to avoid each other after they and Molly's friends are netted with goldfish destined for an indoor tank.

Can the mirlings stay hidden from the humans while surrounded by glass?

Will river-born Grandad end his days in a fish-tank?

Will Flash's recklessness endanger them all?

Will the humans ever master fish-tank maintenance?

Printed in Great Britain
by Amazon